Flight of the Naturne

by A.J.Cunningham

Published by New Generation Publishing in 2014

Copyright © A. J. Cunningham 2014

First Edition

The author asserts the moral right under the Copyright, Designs and Patents Act 1988 to be identified as the author of this work.

All Rights reserved. No part of this publication may be reproduced, stored in a retrieval system or transmitted, in any form or by any means without the prior consent of the author, nor be otherwise circulated in any form of binding or cover other than that which it is published and without a similar condition being imposed on the subsequent purchaser.

www.newgeneration-publishing.com

 New Generation **Publishing**

To
Auntie Louise

The perfect chaperone on a night out ~~

lots of love

A Thompson

This book is dedicated to Tonie Lauren Blackmore, the first one to read this book and say it was something special.

<Chapter 1>

The Baby in the Basket.

On a mountain, far off in the deep regions of Britain, a storm was raging. In the flashes of lightning jagged rocks, like the teeth of a Griffin, could be seen. The bitter cold pricked at everything it touched. The wind brought with it the screams of distant women that hung in the surrounding air.

Far off, in the distance, a Pegasus with a glossy chestnut coat was flying towards the mountain. A man in a black cloak was on its back. His hood was up to protect him from the pelting rain.

The Pegasus flew closer to the mountain and gracefully landed in a clearing free of rocks. The man dismounted from the Pegasus, petting its nose in gratitude.

"Good boy," he said to his steed in a deep Scottish accent, "There, there. Now you wait here and I'll be back soon."

The man slowly walked away from the Pegasus. He reached the middle of the clearing, stopped, reached up a frost bitten hand, and slowly lowered the hood of his cloak.

Straight away the rain attacked his shiny, billowing, shoulder length black hair. His lively hazel-brown eyes scanned the clearing. They seemed to be looking for something. The already strong wind blew itself into a gale and started to whip at the man's cloak.

Alfred Pine walked back to his Pegasus.

"Well Hazelnut, I guess all we can do is wait." The Pegasus gave a low whine. "Don't worry, I will be home and you in a warm stable, soon enough." Alfred said, once again petting Hazelnut affectionately.

The rain was steadily getting heavier. From the other side of the clearing a small flicker of light could be seen through the darkness, only distinguished from the flashes of lighting due to the yellow warmth of its light. Like a candle's flame extinguished by a breeze, the light disappeared.

Alfred walked, almost hesitantly, towards where he had last seen the light. He was nearing the edge of the clearing. Somewhere behind him Hazelnut neighed with worry for his master, the uneasy atmosphere unnerving him.

A lightning strike lit something up on the ground. The roaring thunder was all Alfred could here. With very little light in the unnaturally dark night, he walked blindly forward.

Suddenly, his foot hit something. The thing he had kicked giggled. In bewilderment, Alfred looked down at his feet. On the floor, in a basket woven from water-reeds, lay a small child bundled in rags. A small child who was smiling up at him. Is this what the note had spoken of?

Earlier that day, although it felt like almost an eternity ago, Alfred had received a roughly written note, on a crumpled piece of paper, by flame mail. It had instructed that if he travelled to the ruins of Ben Nevis he would find something very precious and of great value.

Alfred considered that this must be what the note had meant in the absence of anything else on this barren mountain top. As soon as Alfred came to this conclusion his father's words echoed in his head.

'If you've ruled out the impossible, the improbable, no matter how unlikely, must be the truth.'

Alfred bent down and gingerly picked up the basket. As he did so a corner of a note poked itself out of the blankets. He pulled it out, ripped it open and began to read the untidy scrawl, made even worse by the rain that had the ink running off the page.

Dear Alfred,
I knew I could rely on you to come, even if it was an anonymous
request. This is the daughter of Philon Dream. He killed her mother in anger and for her own safety, I stole her from him. By the time you find this note, I probably would have met my end as well. This child's name is Teara Dream. Philon was going to teach her how to use her hidden magic for his cause. I couldn't let her grow up like that.
I can only hope that by me doing this small act for good, I can be forgiven, for the things I did in aid of Philon's cause.
Thank you...

Alfred stood for a moment staring at the letter in complete shock. He couldn't believe it. Here was the daughter of Philon Dream. One of the most dangerous Wizards in the known world. Yet she seemed so sweet and innocent.

As Alfred looked into Teara's eyes he didn't see a speck of evil in them. On the contrary, he saw only hope, kindness and the innocence only a child oblivious to the horrors of life could hold. Her eyes slowly changed colour, blending from grey, to blue, to green.

According to the Ancient laws eyes that changed colour was supposed to always be a sign of goodness. In all of eternity there had only ever been three cases recorded of changing eyes allied with evil. Could she be the fourth?

Teara's giggle interrupted Alfred's inner turmoil. There was only one thing to do. Alfred put down the basket, Teara still tucked up inside, at his feet again. He would have to use the magic within him.

Alfred took two steps away from the basket. He raised one hand above his head and said loud and clear a spell in the language of old.

He pointed his now glowing hand at Teara. A turquoise blue light shot from his hand towards the basket. Once it connected it engulfed the basket, and Teara, in a bright white light.

Teara looked out of her blanket in puzzlement at the light that was now blocking her view of Alfred. The round light was slowly turning into flames.

Alfred could no longer see Teara, just the white flames that surrounded her. He could hear a muffled giggle coming from within the light. This was certainly not like any child Alfred had seen or heard of before.

Any other child out in a storm, with thunder, rain and wind pounding them from all directions, and strange, white flames surrounding them would be scared or crying by now. Anything but giggling.

The flames were getting smaller. After a couple more minutes had passed they had completely disappeared. Teara was still lying in her basket as if nothing had happened.

For the first time that evening, a smile flickered across Alfred's face. He walked over to the basket and picked it up, more gently this time, with his muscular arms.

The flames had told Alfred all he needed to know. This child, Teara Dream, had a good heart. A heart that was destined for greatness.

"You couldn't be less like your father could you?" Alfred asked Teara, not expecting a reply as, of course, she couldn't possibly reply. Teara turned her head to Alfred.

"You act as though you can understand me!" Alfred

stated, a chuckle at the back if his throat. Teara smiled up at him.

"You know, if I didn't know any better I'd say that you could." The storm was calming down now. The rain had begun to dissipate and the lightning has ceased. The wind no longer carried those screams of distant women. Alfred noticed this.

He was almost positive that those screams were the screams of mothers coming home to find their children dead or gone. Most parents knew not to leave their children alone in these dark times. However for some reason or another it still happened.

Finally, the rain stopped. Teara sneezed and Alfred laughed. His smile plastered on his face. He looked up at the sky. The air was fresh and clear now. The clouds in the sky were a pearly white. The sky slowly turning blue.

The tip of the sun could be seen on the distant horizon. The wind now carried with it a love song, sung by sirens miles away. It was the type of song they sung in rejoice and not to lure sailors to their watery depths. Alfred didn't know what they could possibly have to rejoice about in times as dark as these.

Alfred looked around the clearing. He could see a lot more now the storm had cleared. He could see the cliff where the rest of the mountain used to be before being destroyed by the birth of a stone dragon. He sighed.

"I know I won't be able to look after you myself. I've got an academy to run, not to mention all my other duties. But I will feed you and supply you with all you need. I will teach you all I know. I can tell, just by looking at you, that you have the potential to be a great Witch." He told her.

Teara looked up at him, her eyes changing from green to dark brown.

"I know just the person that would be able to raise you and I'm sure you'll get along with her like a house on fire. Though hopefully not as destructive."

Alfred walked back to where Hazelnut was waiting patiently, a lot calmer now that the storm had passed. Mounting his trusted steed, Alfred instructed, "Bring us home, Hazelnut."

With one flap of the Pegasus' great wings, and a kick of his legs, they smoothly rose into the air and were soon flying off to where Teara would soon call home.

<Chapter 2>

Rosemi

Alfred and Teara were soon nearing the end of their journey. Alfred had once again raised his hood and had wrapped Teara more tightly in her blankets in order to protect her from the slipstream.

Hazelnut glided towards the ground, his hooves lightly skimming the treetops before weightlessly landing on the solid soil, cushioned by the well-tailored lawn. Alfred dismounted from his loyal steed, holding the basket close to his chest. He lifted up his hand to lower his hood once more.

With a smile he gazed up at the magnificent building in front of him. His home and his academy where he trained and taught the next generation. The beautiful mansion was made of red bricks that blazed in the morning sun, reflecting the light back giving any who gazed upon it the impression that it was glowing. Five stories of windows glinted in the light, looking like someone had blown glitter to make the windows shine. The entrance to this haven was a solid red oak door that blended into the brickwork, its only distinctive feature the dark green ivy that climbed along its frame. Granite steps led up to the doorway, making the building look inviting to all. At the bottom of these steps stoop a simple wooden sign declaring:

The Wizard and Witch Academy.
To help you master your Hidden
Magic.

Alfred placed his head on Hazelnut's forehead, smiling as he fed the Pegasus a sugar cube from his pocket. Hazelnut gobbled up his treat, gave Alfred an affectionate head-butt and galloped cheerfully off into the ancient forest that lay at the edge of the academy grounds. Like most great clusters of greenery the forest looked at first dark and forbidding with no light able to penetrate below the canopies of the leaves.

Alfred started to walk away from the field towards the grand house. He walked up the familiar steps and pushed the oak door gently. It obediently opened onto a large room bordered by marble pillars accompanied by a smooth wooden floor. A couple of book cases and tables were propped up against the walls and pictures of history lay dotted around the room. Wooden doors led off in every direction. At the end of the room a grand staircase of marble led up into the other floors. On one side a small marble arch led into what looked like a hall or cafeteria.

It was the staircase that Alfred aimed for. As they climbed they passed more and more corridors, each one with more doors leading to more rooms in what seemed like an endless maze. Soon they had reached the fourth floor. Alfred confidently turned to the corridor on his left and proceeded down.

On the walls were more paintings and pictures of history. Landscapes of iconic places, portraits of dead and gone bureaucrats, leaders and old royalty. Everything from an oil painting of the Giant's Causeway to a photograph of the Houses of Parliament.

As they neared the end of the corridor they were greeted by a normal looking door. It was this door that Alfred slowly opened.

Inside was a traditional teacher's desk adorned in messy paperwork, open books and discarded stationary. The walls were full of shelves, bending from the amount of books piled upon them.

After clearing a space Alfred carefully placed Teara,

still inside her basket, on his desk. He then walked round and sat in the wooden chair that lay on the opposite side.

Once sitting for a moment in thought, Alfred opened the middle drawer of his desk and took out a small emerald. He gripped it tightly in his left hand, closed his eyes and called,

"Rosemi, can I see you for a moment please?"

Suddenly a young women appeared in a spiral of green leaves. She had long, waist length, black hair that shimmered in the steady sunlight emanating from the window. She had dark green eyes that looked like the plush greenery of a rainforest, but sparkled with flecks of silver like dew on the grass. Fitting her like a second skin was a dress made out of autumn leaves. The reds, yellows, oranges and browns of the dress blended together making he look like autumn personified. The mixture of colours brought out her pale skin. She carried around her an aura of safety and calm.

"You called for me." She addressed Alfred, only a hint of curiosity could be heard within her voice.

"Yes. I have something to ask you" Alfred replied.

"And what is it?" She asked, raising an eyebrow in question.

"You see this child?" Alfred waved a hand at Teara in her basket.

Rosemi moved closer to the desk so she could peer into the basket to look at the child within.

"I want you to raise her as her own." Alfred finished, looking at Rosemi's face for any sign of an answer.

Rosemi picked up Teara, cradled her with her arms and took her time before answering. As she thought Teara smiled up at her seeming happy to be out of the confines of her basket.

"But I am a Nymph. And she a human." Rosemi

stated.

"I know. I wouldn't ask this if it wasn't important. But if anyone can raise her right, it's you, and I simply am not ready to be a parent. You are much older and wiser than me, I'm sure you've had a lot more experience in the matters of raising a child. You have much to teach her."

"Experience nor age can equate to a good parent. Anyone can raise a child, it is just a matter of following your instincts and hoping that they lead you the right way. However, I cannot help but wonder if this child can be trusted. I can sense something strange about her." Rosemi implied.

"She can. I used the judgement spell on her, the light turned bright white. It showed me that she is destined for greatness." Alfred told her, a grin flashing across his handsome face.

"Her heart may be good but that does not mean it can't be tainted. What's her name?"

"She's called Teara Dream. She's the......."

"You mean she's the daughter of one of the Dream brothers!" Rosemi interrupted him, anger flashing momentarily across her face. "Have you heard the news on Philon?" Rosemi sat in the chair opposite Alfred.

"No. What's happened now?" he asked in a resigned, aspirated voice.

"He's given up. Gone over to America. Taken all his recruits with him by the looks of it." Rosemi said replacing Teara carefully into her basket.

"He won't be gone long. You're holding his daughter"

"So that is her father. Then she has a hard life ahead of her. But for the moment Philon has left this country. Life can now return back to normal."

"I don't think he's gone for good. He wouldn't give up that quickly. He'll be back. I'm sure of it." Alfred clenched his fist.

"He'll most certainly be back. You don't expect him to be away forever when his daughter's still here," Rosemi stated, waving her hand at Teara. "Even someone as evil as him must hold some emotion for his flesh and blood. However, back to the matter in hand, if I do take her, will she be living in the forest with me? And what are the conditions?" Rosemi asked. Her face betraying no emotion, giving no clue on whether she would foster the child or not.

"I wish for her to come here at least twice a day for meals, and sleep in a bedroom on the top floor. She will also come to me three times a week for schooling, at all other times I wish for her to be in your care, at least for the time being."

"And what do you mean by 'for the time being'" Rosemi asked gravely.

"I mean that when she can talk, understand life around her and make rational decisions, I will let her make some decisions for herself, and I will respect her choices. It is best to learn how to choose ones path from an early age, not be mollycoddled then left floundering without knowing how to use one's own devices." He explained.

"Wise words from one with no parenting experience. You must know that, if I agree to this, she might not be like other Witches and Wizards. She might pick up some Nymph powers from living with us from such a young age. She will, more than likely, be more close to nature than any other human alive today. She will be taught how to respect the people, creatures and nature all around her. The culture and lives that nymphs live will be opened up to her in such a way that hasn't been seen in thousands of years. This will impact the way her magic grows and develops. Though I am sure you will not disagree to this." Rosemi concluded, smiling for the first time that evening. Her smile was warm and comforting, it lit up the room.

"No. I will not disagree with you. She will be safe in the Luna forest, won't she?"

"She will be as safe as we are in this room. Probably more." Rosemi reassured him.

Teara giggled in her basket. Any other child probably wouldn't know that these two adults were discussing their future. But then again, Teara Dream, was no ordinary child. She may not understand what Alfred and Rosemi were saying, but somehow she knew it was about her and what was to become of her.

"When would you want me to take her into my care? I know you have an academy to run. And with recent developments, I am positive a meeting will be called to discuss the changes that will come now that the Dream Squad have left." Rosemi inquired.

"Now. If you wouldn't mind." Alfred nodded.

Rosemi got up and gently picked Teara up out of her basket, cradling her in her arms once more.

"Rosemi, before you go. There was this note in the basket with her. I think you should read it." Alfred held up the soggy note for Rosemi to read.

Once Rosemi had finished she nodded her head to show she understood.

"Rosemi, I don't know how to thank you. This means a lot to me. Ask anything of me and I will do all I can, till my last breath, to do it." Alfred said. He stood up and gave Rosemi a bow.

"I will do my best to help this child. If you need me you know how to reach me."

"Thank you again."

In Rosemi's arms Teara once again giggled. Then closed her eyes and fell into a dreamful sleep. Rosemi and Teara disappeared in the spiral of leaves that was the nymphs was of transportation.

Alfred smiled at himself. It was the beginning of something. He just didn't know what.

15 Years Later

<Chapter 3>

Grown

The sun was steadily rising over the Luna Forest. It's warm, comforting rays descending down, through the tree branches, to the ground below. The birds in the trees singing a beautiful song of spring to greet the new morning.

Teara lay asleep on one of the many high branches of an old oak tree. Her long flowing blond hair, was hanging off the branch swaying in the playful breeze. She was deep asleep, smiling at something that was occurring in her dreams.

A lot had changed since Teara had been found by Alfred on the ruins of Ben Nevis all those years ago. She had learnt how to shiver, the Nymph's equivalent of transportation, something unheard of for many generations, as well as control her hidden magic.

Teara had begun to stir when she was awoken very abruptly. She looked down to the ground below. There, at the base of the tree was a pure white unicorn. It's horn a perfect spiral and it's white coat reflecting the sunlight, giving it the appearance of it glowing. It had a hoof raised as if it was about to kick the tree.

"No wait!" Teara shouted down to it. A smile flickered across her face. She slid of the branch, and scurried down the tree like a monkey, and jumped the last few feet, landing perfectly upright. Teara walked over to the unicorn, smiling as she did so.

"I suppose it was you who woke me up, Spirit." She said playfully.

"*You told me to wake you.*" Spirit's voice entered Teara's mind. Teara shared a special connection with this unicorn. When she was five she was playing with Spirit, at which time he was only a little foal, no older than a month old colt. In the middle of their playful antics, Spirit's horn erupted out of his head. Then his voice filled Teara's mind.

Only she could understand him in this way. As, if you bore witness to a unicorn birthing its horn, you would share a bond with that unicorn like no other. Ever since the connection had started, Spirit and Teara had been inseparable.

"I know, but I can't remember why." Teara laughed at her own thoughtlessness. "Anyway, I thought you had a meeting with the France herd today."

"*I do. I'm just going to get a drink and then I'll be off.*" Spirit replied.

"I'll join you."

Teara and Spirit walked over to the pond which was at the edge of the clearing. It was a beautiful thing, with a waterfall flowing into it. Behind the waterfall was a cave, where Teara sometimes slept, the sounds of the water crashing into the pond soothing her to sleep. The water was clear and filled with countless minerals, with a fine bed of sand at the bottom.

Spirit bent his neck and drank from the water. Teara cupped her hands and quenched her thirst.

"*Well I've got to go. Bye.*" Spirit said to her before he galloped off into the trees. It looked like he had shimmered over to them, after all unicorns were the fastest creatures alive.

Teara sat by the pond trying to think through the haze sleep had left in her mind so she could remember why she had asked Spirit to wake her up. She stood up. Her Nymph dress catching in the breeze. It like all of the other dresses worn by the nymphs except it was made of green leaves, a sign of her being a young member of the clan.

"Teara."

Startled, Teara turned around to see who had called

her. There, walking towards her was Rosemi. Her black hair hanging down to her waist. She was as young looking as ever and wearing her dress of autumn leaves that marked her as the leader of this clan of Nymphs.

"Good morning Teara. Did you sleep well?" Rosemi asked.

"Yes thank you. Rosemi, do you have any idea why I asked Spirit to wake me up? Because I can't seem to remember why I did."

"Could it be because you've only been to the Academy twice this week, and it is now a Friday? You did say you would go at least three times a week."

Teara brought her hand to her forehead, shocked at her own forgetfulness.

"That must be it. Thanks. Hey Rosemi, guess what?" Teara asked as an afterthought.

"Do I want to guess?"

"We've only got two more weeks and then we've got holidays" Teara was jumping up and down on the spot.

"And you'll do what you always do. Staying in the forest, swimming, being you, and getting on my last nerve."

"Yep!"

"Hmm. Right, well first of all get some breakfast and then get changed into your uniform." Rosemi sighed, and gestured a hand at Teara's clothes.

"OK." Teara went behind one of the small wooden huts that surrounded the pond. These huts were where the Nymphs lived. They were made of old branches found around the forest, and seemed to admit a magical aurora that hung around them.

Teara came back from behind the huts wearing a black skirt, which reached to just above her knee, and a black shirt, with W.W.A in gold letters on it. Teara walked back over to Rosemi.

"Changed," Teara announced giving a twirl.

"Yes. Now get your breakfast." Rosemi reminded her before she could forget. Teara closed her eyes, picturing buttered toast, with a thin layer of jam in her mind. When she opened her eyes, low and behold, there, floating in mid-air, was a piece of buttered toast, just as she had imagined. Teara took it up and started to eat.

"It's really unnerving when you do that. I can't remember the last time I saw a human use our powers so effectively." Rosemi told her, shaking her head in disbelief.

"Oy I Ualt." Teara said through her toast. She swallowed.

"Sorry. I said, it's not my fault that I can use them. And it's not like I know all of them, just the basic few. The nymphs younger than me can do so much more than I can" Teara stated, with a hint of jealousy in her voice.

"True, but that's still more than any human can at this present moment in time. And there is no need to hold such jealousy for those younger than you. All you do is waste energy creating that envy, you must remember that they are born with the powers where as you have to learn them." Rosemi replied. She looked at Teara in a motherly sort of way.

"Still when Alfred and I found you, we knew you were no ordinary person. You never cried. No matter how much the thunder roared or the wind howled. You just giggled and acted as though nothing was wrong. And all this time I've known you. You've never cried. No matter how much you got hurt. You just got up, brushed yourself off and carried on."

"What can I say? I've got no tear ducts." Teara pointed to her eyes then burst out laughing. Rosemi gave a small smile and shook her head. No matter what, this girl always seemed to find something to laugh at. It was like she was determined to always see the light side.

"You've also got no grades. And you won't have any unless you get going." Rosemi told her.

"Alright, alright." Teara said laughing. "I've just got to get my bag."

"And where would that be?" Rosemi asked, her hands on her hips.

"Up in the tree. I'll go get it." Teara ran over to the same oak tree she had awoken in that morning. There, hanging on a branch, was her bag. She jumped onto the nearest branch and started to climb. In no time at all she had reached her bag. She put it over her shoulder and climbed back down. When Teara reached the bottom, she walked back over to Rosemi.

"I got it. I'll be off. See you after lessons." Teara said nonchalantly.

"After lessons." Rosemi nodded. "Oh and Teara."

"Yes."

"Walk. It'll do you good." Rosemi smiled again.

"OK." Teara walked towards the rarely used deer trail that would lead her out of the clearing, through the trees, and to the academy to begin her day.

<Chapter 4>

A morning walk

Soon, Teara was surrounded by the old trees of the forest. Unnerved, she carried on walking down the trail. Somewhere in the distance the sounds of a Griffin's scream reached her. Years ago the scream would have scared Teara to bits, but now she was no longer scared. Now she knew that this scream was not of the creature hunting, nor was it that sound of that the creature intended her harm. It was the scream of joy a Griffin made when some unexpected joy came its way. It was knowledge like this, learnt through living in the forest that calmed Teara. Things that would scare someone who knew nothing of the workings of the forest only brought her calm and a sense of normality. It also helped that it had always taken a lot to make her feel unnerved, a trait many said she received from her father.

Teara didn't know much about her father. Whenever she broached the subject with Alfred or Rosemi she was stonewalled, receiving only one word answers and subject changes. All she knew was that he was a great Wizard, but had a very evil personality. He had tried to get The Clans, (people who couldn't and/or wouldn't use their Hidden magic), and mythical creatures put in isolation. No one knew why he had wanted this, and as far as she knew no one had even bothered to look for his motives. Like many things in the past it has simply been brushed under the carpet.

She wasn't proud to be his daughter, but she wasn't ashamed either. Teara couldn't help this matter of her heritage and so she has learned from a young age to accept it.

Teara pushed these thoughts to the back of her head, trying to stop the cloud of darkness and depression that often descended with them. Instead deciding to focus on the trial, observing the forest going through its morning ritual. She saw mamma birds feeding there young, a squirrel running along a branch, and as she looked up she noticed an owl settling down for its days' rest.

The green leaves on the trees rustled in the breeze that playfully weaved through the branches. Teara stopped and looked up in wonder at how the sunlight glinted through the canopy above her. No matter how many times she looked, it always amazed her at how so much light could penetrate through such a thick layer of leaves. Many people believed that the forest was a dark place, if she didn't know any better she would believe it too.

Teara carried on her way, her thoughts turning to the day ahead. She wondered what they would be learning in lesson today. Last week Teara's class had learned about the Spiral Attack. It was an attack that could create a mini twister. The twister could trap someone or something inside it, though she did have trouble pronouncing the spell. The idea of the spell was that while the thing or person was trapped inside, you could escape or plan your next attack. However, knowing the purpose of a spell didn't help with pronouncing the words that put it into action.

As Teara continued to walk through the forest she saw a variety of all different creatures. She saw a couple more owls, a few centaurs that galloped past in the distance, a group of unicorns, no doubt on their way to the meeting with the herd from France and even a Kacheeka.

A Kacheeka was a small animal that grew to be only a foot high. They could sense if you were kind or frightened to meet them, or even if you were going to hurt them. In times past these small creatures were often mistaken for fairies or elves, though now people knew that there were many mythical creatures that had emerged when people discovered that they had hidden magic within them.

Kacheekas were a shy type of animal that would try to keep out of a fight, and would gladly make friends with anything. Kacheekas could be a variety of colours, depending on the mood they were in, like a chameleon. They had pointed ears, that were often lopsided, and only had two toes on each of their feet. They had a very small tail and their fur was short and soft. When Teara spotted the Kacheeka she only got a quick glimpse before it scurried into the undergrowth. Even though she didn't mean them any harm, these creatures still preferred to be unseen and to keep their own company.

Teara was now beginning to near the end of the path. More and more light was filtering through the trees, whose canopy had begun to thin. The tree trunks were becoming further and further apart, and were becoming thinner, showing they were the younger trees of the old forest.

As Teara reached the end of the trail a bolt of noise hit her. The sounds of children chatting, laughing and playing filled the air. *It must be nearly lesson time*, Teara thought.

As it was Friday Teara only had one lesson, and that was Power Studies. A class where she would learn the spells that would harness her hidden magic and project, mould and contain it into a physical form. It was her favourite lesson her mind never had a chance to drift, though she wished the words used for the spells were a lot easier to speak.

Teara crossed the field and joined the crowd of children that was flooding into the red brick mansion which stood at the top of five, beautifully carved, granite steps.

As Teara entered the academy her blue eyes scanned the crowd, looking for her best friend. Teara spotted her over by one of the pillars, making balls of light appear out of the palm of her hand. Her face was scrunched up in concentration, a line forming between her brows.

Teara smiled and crept over.

"I don't think it needs any more light in here." She said loudly and the girl jumped.

"You startled me." The girl said before joining Teara in her laughter. The two girls hugged each other.

"Hi Sophelia. How are you?" Teara asked.

"Oh I'm fine, or at least I was till this weirdo decided I could live with my heart in my throat! You?"

"I'm good." Teara smiled at the girl whom shared her humour.

Sophelia had short ginger hair whose curls only just scraped her shoulders, which really complemented her perfect heart shaped face. She also had deep red lips and light green eyes, which reminded Teara of freshly mown grass. There was also a light speckling of freckles over her nose.

"You weren't in yesterday. I missed you" Sophelia stated.

"I went over to Plymouth with the Banshees." Teara replied.

"That must have been fun, though it sounds like you didn't scream yourself hoarse. You missed History, Sports and Power Studies, you lucky girl!"

"Yeah," Teara said, "Pity I missed Power Studies. But you know I hate History and I don't need Sports."

"I wish I didn't, running around the field is not attractive. In fact running at all isn't attractive full stop. Come on, we better get a move on or else we're going to be late." Sophelia sighed.

Sophelia and Teara walked up the staircase, heading to the third floor where the Power Studies class was held. They had almost passed the second floor when Sophelia spotted Calumeno and instantly froze.

Calumeno was a guy that Sophelia had a huge crush on. He had short, spiky brown hair and blue eyes, that in Sophelia's words 'you could just drown in'. He was about five foot four and as had been stated by Sophelia many times 'was the perfect height for her!'

A bright red blush had started to creep up Sophelia's face. As it reached her nose Teara grabbed her arm and pulled.

"Come on, before you turn into a beetroot."

Teara dragged her friend up the stairs, Sophelia staring until Calumeno was out of sight.

Teara snapped her fingers in front of Sophelia's eyes, and waved her hand back and forth across Sophelia's face, which was still staring down the staircase.

"Hello. Anyone in there?"

"Sorry Teara. How bad was it?" Sophelia asked, snapping out of her daydream.

"Not bad. You were just as lovesick as a puppy."

"That bad!" Sophelia sounded surprised.

"Ahuh. I still don't know what you see in him. I mean he is just a guy."

"He's just sooooooo dreamy. Don't you think so?"

"Hmm. Last time I checked. NO!" Sophelia and Teara laughed.

"Come on. Better get going."

Teara and Sophelia carried on up the stairs to the third floor. Once they reached the landing they turned left, down into another corridor. They strolled down it and entered the second door to their right.

The class room was full of tables that could have two people sitting at each of them. There was a desk by a white board but other than that the room was sparsely decorated. This was due to the fact of powers being learnt. With little furniture there would be less damage and less time wasted on moving things out of the way.

More and more children wearing the W.W.A uniform came into the class. The boys wearing shorts instead of skirts. Though the uniform was compulsory, there was no strict way of wearing it. Therefore many people had individualised their uniforms, some by adding accessories and others by changing how they wore it.

The two friends had just taken a table in the middle of the class, settled themselves down when a boy with messy blond hair ran into the class saying,

"The teachers coming."

In one swift moment everyone was in their seats and were silent. Students knew better than to cause trouble in academy where the teachers could literally turn you into a frog.

<Chapter 5>

Pure Heart Shield

The whole class now lay in silence. The air full with anticipation for their teacher, and for the new power they were to learn. Footsteps could be heard coming down the corridor, their sound getting louder the closer they got to the door until their teacher walked through the door smiling at his class.

Before greeting his pupils, Alfred walked over to his desk and unloaded the notes and books he had been carrying. Since the time he had found Teara, age had come into play, his handsome face now held wrinkles of wisdom and laughter lines, below his eyes, crow's feet had begun to form, and a few stray grey hairs had appeared in his otherwise black hair.

"Good morning, class." he addressed the students before him, a bright smile spread across his face at the predicted reply.

"Good morning Mr. Pine."

Alfred looked over the class, mentally taking the register, when his gaze landed on Teara he gave her a small nod in greeting which she promptly returned.

"Well class, today, we are learning how to use the Pure Heart Shield. Does anyone know what this power does?"

A boy with messy brown hair at the back of the class put his hand up. His sleeves riding up his arms, showing that his uniform was too small for him. Once Alfred had acknowledged him, the student spoke.

"It's a type of shield sir. It is designed to protect you" A cheeky grin spread across his face, his eyes twinkling with a hint of mischief. In response to his answer he was rewarded with a roll of the eyes and a smile from his teacher, whilst the rest of the class laughed.

"Yes Brandon, it's a type of shield, but does anyone know what it is specifically used to defend against?" Alfred again looked around the class.

Teara had an idea, after all she had spent her whole life reading the academic books in the school, but she was marginalised enough for the circumstances in which she lived, and so decided to keep quiet in the hope that she could blend into the student body as another average pupil.

"No-one?" Alfred sighed, he had hoped at least one of his students would have done some research. "OK, as Brandon already pointed out, a shield is used to protect oneself from danger. However, a Pure Heart Shield can be used to protect its caster from any power that's purpose is to harm anyone, it may not protect against one that is to cause death, but that depends entirely on the situation. After all no magic is definite."

A girl with shoulder length black hair in the middle row put her hand up, her hand was shaking with nerves, but her curiosity had gotten the best of her.

"Yes Alicia."

"Why does it depend on the situation? Will we learn something that can guarantee our safety?" Alicia asked.

"A very good question Alicia. It depends on the situation as this particular spell moulds your hidden magic into the feeling that has consumed you heart. It then makes this feeling physical by solidifying your feeling in the form as a shield. A shield that would guarantee your protection is almost unheard of, however when you reach the upper years, and your magic has matured a bit more, you will be taught the spells to mould your magic into more powerful forms."

"What type of things could this shield protect against?" Alicia asked Alfred. The class leaned forwards in their seats in anticipation, wanting to know the answer.

"This particular shield will protect against something like a pain blast. I've never had to experience its effects. However I have heard that the pain starts in your heart and moves out-wards until your whole body is consumed. And before you ask, no, I will not tell you the words to be spoken to use it." Alfred told the class sternly.

In response to the knowledge that had just been imparted to them a couple of students raised their hands up. Alfred answered their questions quickly and one at a time, trying to move onto the main purpose of the lesson, but at the same time happy that they wanted to learn. One of them wanted to know if they would be ever learn the words that would create a pain blasts.

Alfred calmly told them they'd only be taught it in there very last year, under very, very tight conditions.

One of the other questions was whether Alfred knew anyone who had suffered the effects of the pain blast, in reply the student was told that he did, but any such stories would be left unheard till they had matured.

The last question asked was from a small girl with brown hair neatly tied up in a bun at the back of her head, sitting in the front row.

"Does it matter what feelings you have when you cast the shield?" She asked.

"Yes," Alfred replied, "the stronger the feeling, the stronger the shield, for example a fickle feeling like jealousy or bewilderment would produce a weak shield, but strong feelings such as love or hate will produce. This spell is one of the few where many feelings can be used to solidify the magic, such spells like the pain blast require only one of a few feelings, such as distaste, to make it work."

The class looked at each other and burst into

whispers. Students turned to one another, discussing which feelings they thought were strongest. Alfred thought he would leave his students to discuss the knowledge he had just imparted for a little while, before he carried on with the lesson. He was a great believer in discussion helping to keep the lessons taught within a person's mind for longer.

Sophelia leaned over to talk to Teara.

"I'd never heard anything like a pain blast before, Have you?"

"I have heard of it." Teara replied in a small voice, the dark thoughts of this morning's walk and of her father returning to her mind. If she recalled correctly her father had been famous for using such magic.

"Oh Teara, I'm so sorry I forgot."

"Don't worry Soph, it doesn't bother me anymore." Teara quickly reassured her friend, turning away so she wouldn't see her eyes changing colour at the lie she had just spoke.

"OK quieten down now please." The class slowly regained its silent state.

"Now that we've all had time to discuss what we just learnt I think it's time we all moved on with the lesson. Now as we all should know by now we are learning how to use the Pure Heart Shield. If everyone could please help to push the tables and chairs back, I think we can begin."

The sounds of furniture scraping the floor filled the room, as the class got out of their seats, and pushed their tables and chairs back against the farthest wall in a rehearsed manner. Each one eager to move on to practical work.

"Ok first of all I believe I will have to tell you the words needed to instigate your powers. The words you will need are *ion chroi cosain*. Make sure you pronounce it properly and you shouldn't have any problem. Although I will give you a demonstration."

"OK then. First of all you cross your arms over your chest. Focus on what you want, in this case a shield to protect you, try and think of a memory that made you really happy. When you feel you are completely focused, uncross your arms. As you do this, you must say the incantation on *ion chroi cosain*. However you must say it with feeling and the movement of your arms should be fluent. The gestures should flow into each other, so it looks like one graceful movement. Do you understand?"

Once Alfred was sure the class had understood he stepped back from the class and followed his own instructions.

After a pause he began to focus and when he had grabbed the memory of his choosing he held it tightly in his mind, as he did so a pink light came out from where his hands were crossed. Before the magic could burst into sparkles he said the incantation that would turn the magic into a physical presence. No sooner than the words *ion chroi cosain* had left his mouth a bright pink bubble formed in front of him, creating a shield like shape.

The class gave gasps of wonder and awe. After about a minute or so of letting his students study what a fully formed shield looked like, Alfred released the happy memory and in doing so the shield dissolved.

"As I said previously the Pure Heart Shield will protect you from all minor attacks. But if your opponent decides to use anything like a pain blast or a type of Death Blow, the shield will not hold and simply dissolve. In short this is simply something to help you learn to control your magic and to be used to protect you against small, minor attacks. Understand?" Alfred informed his pupils.

The class nodded. Slowly growing impatient with

the anticipation that burned inside each one of them.

"Well what are you waiting around for then? Everyone move to a clear space and start practising the Pure Heart Shield."

The class obediently did as they were told, all excited about learning this new technique that would help them control the magic within them and that could possibly save their life one day.

Sophelia and Teara stood a reasonable distance away from each other, about a meter apart, and started to practice.

Soon the room was full of children saying, "*ion chroi cosain.*" Not all of the students were pronouncing the strange words properly and thus it was almost an hour till any shield became even remotely physical.

Teara was the third person who managed to form a perfect shield. The second was Alicia, who was very shy but a hard worker, and the first was Brandon. For all his mischievous ways and joking behaviour he really was a good student, and probably the brightest on in the class.

After a while some more students managed to complete the task. And just as the end of the lesson was nearing, Sophelia finally created the Pure Heart Shield. She laughed in amazement at it before her lack of concentration led to the shield dissolving into pink sparks.

Alfred stood up from his desk, where he had been watching his class' progress whilst doing some lesson plans, and started to walk around the room, correcting the pupils techniques where needed and reiterating the pronunciation of the words.

"Right class. First of all I'd like you to put the tables and chairs back in their original positions please." Alfred ordered, bringing the students back to earth.

Once his students had completed the task and

returned to their seats, Alfred began to dismiss them.

"OK. Well done for today. I am very impressed with the class progress and attitude towards learning this new power. I'm happy to say that most of you picked it up quite quickly, even if some of you needed help with your speaking, but for the others I'm afraid you'll be getting a bit of homework. And that is to practice."

There was a moan from some of the class whilst the rest smiled, glad to have an evening off, although they more than likely would try the spell again.

"Class dismissed. Remember to bring your Ringtons in on Monday, and Teara, if possible I would like to have a word with you after the class has gone please. Alfred finished.

The class started to disperse out of the door.

"I'll wait for you outside, OK." Sophelia told Teara, giving her a hand of quick squeeze. She then walked out of the door too. When the classroom was empty of all but Alfred and Teara, Alfred quietly closed the door.

<Chapter 6>

Vinnie

After he had closed the door, Alfred returned to sit in his chair.

"Teara, pull up a chair."

As quickly as she could, Teara pulled a chair over from a nearby table, placed it in front of Alfred's desk and sat down. She tilted her head, giving Alfred an inquisitorial look, making it clear that she had no idea why he had wanted to talk to her.

"Teara, is there any point in me having set aside a couple of rooms for your own private use when you don't use them. More times than I can count, I've gone up to talk to you and your bed is unslept, the curtains closed and every side is covered in dust! Why is that?" Alfred sighed, reclining in his seat.

"Because you said I could sleep outside if I want to..." Teara drawled off, knowing that she had just resurrected an argument that was as old as she was.

"I know I did. But I thought that I also told you that I would like you to sleep inside during the winter season." Alfred stated.

"Actually, you said you'd *prefer* it if I slept indoors." Teara replied.

Alfred rolled his eyes, "Teara, I know you like it out there, but you do not have the same type of immune system as the nymphs, if it gets much colder then you could get hypothermia or worse."

"Technically it's not winter it's autumn. So it's alright for me to sleep outside." Teara pointed out, completely ignoring Alfred's argument on her getting too cold, after all that's what blankets and jumpers were for.

Alfred took a deep breath. He remained silent for a while. After a sigh of resignation, he spoke.

"You like it in the forest, don't you?" It wasn't phrased as a question but Teara felt that she needed to answer anyway.

"Very much," Teara smiled at the person who was her father figure, a smile which he returned with a shake of his head.

"Well if you like it so much I suppose my points become invalid. You can continue doing as you wish as long as you have your meals in here. Can we agree on that?"

"Um...Well...You see..." Teara stammered.

"You didn't have breakfast did you?" Alfred shook his head.

"Well...Yeah...I did have breakfast...but I kinda, maybe, possibly, didn't have it in here."

"I get the feeling that I am fighting a lost cause here. Let's negotiate, you have to have at least two meals from the cafeteria, the other you can have wherever, and whenever you like. Can we at least agree on that?"

"I suppose I can. But Alfred, I don't know why you don't like the forest. It's a wonderful place."

"I just...It's...You never know what might be in there. There could be Ielele."

"Well of course there are Ielele. And their quite friendly actually. All those storied about people dying around them is just propaganda." Teara contradicted him, "And I can take care of myself. I thought you knew that."

"I do. It's just that I worry about you."

"I know you do, but you're the one that's been teaching me for years on how to use my hidden magic. Plus you had me trained in the martial arts after you heard about that serial killer going around all those years ago."

Alfred smiled at Teara. Even though he had never asked to be a parent, this girl, the one that had slowly became like a daughter to him, made him feel the shock that one day all parents would feel. The shock when the realisation hits you that your little girl is starting to get older, she doesn't need you to pick her up when she falls, because now she knows how to do it for herself. Blinking his emotion away from his eyes, Alfred answered her.

"Fine. I'll let you stay in the forest as long as you promise you'll be careful."

Alfred looked into Teara's eyes. Awaiting for her answer. Knowing that if she lied he could tell by her eyes. As soon as a lie left her lips their colour would change.

Teara know this so the few occasions she did lie she hid her face as much as possible, unfortunately she couldn't use that tactic to lie to Alfred, she had learnt that at a young age and had simply learnt how to speak enough of the truth to get by.

"I Promise." Teara said. Her eyes did not change colour and she did not try to hide her face. Alfred sat back, content with her answer.

"Is that all you wanted to talk to me about?" Teara asked. She couldn't see why a conversation like the one they had just had could not have waited till Alfred's busy school day was over. In order for him to ask her to stay behind there would have to be an important or urgent reason.

"Oh yes. I almost forgot." Alfred reached down and opened the middle drawer of his desk. He pulled out a folded newspaper and handed it to her. Teara unrolled it.

"Isn't this the *Wizard Weekly*?" Teara asked, confused as to why Alfred would have handed her a newspaper.

"Yes it is. I want you to read the article on page nineteen and you have to read it while you are alone. Preferably, and I can't believe I am actually saying this, but in the forest." Alfred instructed her.

"Can Sophelia read it with me? I really don't like keeping stuff from her."

"OK. But no-one else. Now you'd better get off to lunch." Alfred said, resting his hand upon her shoulder, smiling down at her.

"But I don't have any more lessons. So I won't be late for anything." Teara replied returning his smile.

"No, but all the food will be gone soon." Alfred stood up and opened the door for her. There waiting outside, leaning against the opposite wall was Sophelia.

"OK, see you later Alfred." Teara got up, put the newspaper in the small pocket of her skirt and walked out of the door to where Sophelia was waiting. The door shut behind her. The two girls started to walk back down the corridor. When they had reached the staircase and had started to descend, Sophelia spoke, letting her eagerness overflow.

"So what did he want?" she tried to sound nonchalant.

"Who?" Teara asked confused, she had been lost in her own thoughts.

"The rock spirit. Who do you think?" Sophelia's voice dripped with sarcasm that brought a smile to both of their faces.

"Oh the usual. Doesn't want me to sleep in the forest, eat my meals indoors and to give me a newspaper to read alone." Teara said very casually.

"Oh OK." Sophelia paused. "Wait. He gave you a newspaper to read alone. Which one? *The Clan Express*? *The Daily Witch*?"

"Whoa! Calm down. No, it was the *Wizard Weekly*." Teara said laughing.

"That one, you know what I don't understand? I don't understand why it's called the *Wizard Weekly* if it's sold twice a week. Anyway. Why did he give you the paper?" Sophelia asked.

"He told me to read the article on page nineteen alone. Preferably in the forest. Oh and he said you could read it with me." Teara told her.

"That's alright then, but let's wait until after lunch. I'm starving..."

Teara laughed, "Sophelia Jenkings, you are always starving."

They were now crossing the threshold into the large hall, which was used as a cafeteria for the students to have their meals.

As Sophelia and Teara entered the hall they were hit by the smells of freshly cooked food, deafened by the sounds of hundreds students talking, and enveloped in a crowd of youngsters running to friends already sat at tables whilst juggling trays full of food.

They walked to one side of the hall to pick up a tray, and then some dinner. They each got a piece of cottage pie and a bottle of juice. They then walked down one of the rows to find seats in the already full to the brim hall. Each of these tables could seat six people. After a couple minutes of searching they managed to find some. The two girls sat down and ate their dinner in companionable silence.

Just as they were finishing they heard a snide voice from above.

"Oh look what the cats dragged in. A couple of starving nerds."

Teara and Sophelia looked up. There standing over them was a girl with curly, mousy brown hair and dark blue eyes. Her nose was stuck up in the air like she had just smelt a field full of manure. Her eyes were looking down at the two girls like they were beneath her. Either side of her was two more girls. Each with matching shoulder length black hair. All in all there was very little difference between them seeing as they were twins.

"What do you three want?" Sophelia asked, resigned to the petty insults that were about to roll, and the sentences that never seemed to be restricted to one person.

"What we want..." one of the twins started.

"Is for you..." The other twin continued.

"To give up on Calumeno." The mousy haired girl finished.

"Not going to happen Vinnie. I allowed to like whoever I want and until he gets a girlfriend I've got as good a chance as anyone else." Sophelia replied.

"Well why would he have you when he can have Vinnie?" One of the twins sniped.

"Ha Vinnie Stocksworthy and Calumeno Price. That just rings wedding bells." Teara laughed.

"You watch it Teara Dream. One of these days you're not going to have your little Nymph friends to protect you." Vinnie snarled.

"Well last time I checked Teara didn't have a Nymph guard following her around." Sophelia snapped.

"No but she does have that necklace." Vinnie pointed to the green necklace that was around Teara's neck. It had a little piece of green sea glass dangling off the chain.

"Everyone knows that all she needs to do is grab that thing, say a stupid Nymph's name and they'll come running." Vinnie finished.

Teara smiled and shook her head, deciding to raise above it. "Vinnie, Vinnie. You wouldn't know a Nymph if it came up and shook your hand. Nymphs don't run. If they need to get somewhere quickly they shiver." Teara stated.

"Dork." The twins said together.

"It's no surprise that you three still know words from last millennium." Sophelia replied.

"Uh, well it's so typical that you two still wear clothes from before the Romans." Vinnie snapped. Thinking on her feet was not her greatest feature.

"Don't you three have anything better to do?" Teara asked, still keeping calm, if anything becoming bored with the tennis match of insults.

"We only came over..."

"To tell her to stay away from Calumeno." The twins split the sentence between them, glaring at Sophelia.

"Not that she stands a chance anyway." Vinnie grinned.

Sophelia stuck out her tongue, whist the twins continues there glares.

"Come on Trix, you too Wanda. If we hurry we might get seats next to Calumeno." Vinnie said to the twins.

They turned their backs on Teara and Sophelia and walked out.

"As nice as always." Sophelia stated and Teara laughed, trying not to spit out her juice. As they finished their drinks, they carried on chatting about how 'Out of order' and 'Stuck up' Vinnie and the twins had been. After all, Sophelia was right, she stood as good a chance of any of winning Calumeno.

<Chapter 7>

The Wizard Weekly

It wasn't soon after that the school bell rang, signalling the end of lunch. Teara and Sophelia picked up their dishes, walked to the opposite end of the cafeteria and placed them on the table to be cleaned. They then joined the large group of students who were walking back along the rows of tables and out of the hall. However, instead of following the flow up the stairs to return to lessons, the two girls headed through the oak doors until they were outside, being blinded by the shining afternoon sun.

"Take a good look, for that won't last much longer." Sophelia said waving to the clear sky. Teara giggled. Sophelia was someone who was naturally funny almost all of the time. Her humour wasn't just from her bright personality but also from her talent of pointing out the obvious. For she was right, the closer winter crept forward, the more cloudy skies there was. As they were walking towards one of the benches, Teara broached the subject about the newspaper in her pocket.

"Sophelia, would you like to go to one of the Nymph's huts and see what Alfred was talking about? You know, in the *Wizard Weekly*. It's just I know everyone is in lessons, but there are still a couple of students dotted around and I'd rather be completely alone."

"OK, that sounds like a good idea, but how are we going to get there? You know I hate walking through the forest, it gives me the heeby jeebies."

"Easy, we ride."

"We what?" Sophelia said looking confused, and slightly worried.

"We ride." Teara said simply.

"On what? The wind? I don't know if you've noticed but the stables are off limits to all students. And if you think I'm flying on a Pegasus, you're wrong. Me and heights just don't mix."

"No silly. Close though. On Spirit. He's not quite a Pegasus but he has his own magical abilities." Teara shook her head at her friend. Their walking had now brought them to the boundary of the field where the forest started. The boundary wasn't official it was just where the well-manicured lawn gave way to occasional shrubs, that in turn led to saplings of baby trees, and after that lay the fully grown trees that stood at the beginning of the Luna forest.

Teara stopped, looking up in awe, wonder and happiness at the large forest that had become like a home to her. Sophelia on the other hand, looked at the forest warily, she could get used to the idea of Teara loving a place like this, and she just couldn't for the life of her understand why anyone would.

"Oh yeah, your unicorn. Will it let me ride it?" Sophelia asked, hoping the answer would be no.

"He should do...he should be here in a min."

"B-but how did he know we were here?"

"I called him." Teara replied simply.

"Well... that makes sense." Sophelia rolled her eyes, secretly confused but not wanting to say anything.

In the distance galloping could be heard. It only took a couple seconds for the two girls to see the white blur exiting the forest. Then Sophelia's gasp made Teara turn around. There, standing next to Sophelia was the pure white unicorn Teara had last seen that morning. The unicorn was sniffing at Sophelia, someone he had heard lots about but had never met up close.

"So this is Spirit!" Sophelia stated. She patted

Spirit's neck. "He seems friendly enough." She said.

"*Is she trying to say I'm dangerous? She's the one who's dressed like a carrot! And she wants to enter the forest looking like that? She'll be eaten in moments!*" Spirit's voice entered Teara's head and she laughed.

"What? What's so funny?" Sophelia asked looking slightly worried.

"Nothing just Spirit thinks you look like a carrot." Teara said trying not to laugh.

"Is he taking the micky out of me?" Sophelia asked her short temper starting to rise. Her look of caution turning into a glare.

"No it's probably because of your orange jumper." Teara said pointing at the orange jumper Sophelia had pulled over uniform to protect her from the dropping temperature.

"Oh OK." Sophelia replied, gently patting Spirit's back.

"Shall we go then?" Teara asked.

"Go where?" Sophelia and Spirit asked together.

"The pond of *Tsaoil*, of course."

"*Hop on.*" Spirit replied. Teara walked over to him and in one move jumped up onto his back. She then pulled Sophelia up behind her.

"We're not going to go too fast are we?" Sophelia asked.

Teara laughed, "Sophelia you can't get on a unicorn then ask to go slow. They are the fastest creatures in the world. That's like asking for a chocolate smoothie with no chocolate."

"OK, you know I can't live without chocolate." Sophelia said wrapping her arms around Teara's waste and holding tight, whilst Teara rolled her eyes.

"Spirit, we're ready." Teara said to her friend.

Spirit started to gallop towards the forest. As the darkness of the trees enveloped them, Sophelia gasped.

Everything blurred faster and faster till it looked like they were travelling through a tunnel of green. Sophelia couldn't distinguish anything except from the green of the passing trees and the occasional blot of blue from the sky. After a couple of minutes, they arrived at the pond Teara had drunk from earlier that day. Teara hopped off and helped her friend down.

"Wow! That was amazing. Let's do it again." Sophelia exclaimed, buzzing from the adrenaline.

"*Teara, I have to go. The herd is going for a run and I said I'd be there.*" Spirit told her, apologetically.

"OK, I'll see you later. Thank you." Teara said waving as Spirit rode off into the trees.

"Where's he going?" Sophelia asked her.

"Back to his herd." Teara replied. "Come on. Let's go inside."

They both walked over towards the huts that surrounded the clearing and entered the one on the far right side, which was slightly bigger than all the others and had roses around it's door way.

Inside was a small table, with two matching chairs either side of it. They were made out of what looked like very old wood and had ancient carvings of cats on its back panal. There was a pile of fresh hay on one side of the hut, where the person who lived there slept. Teara walked over to one of the chairs and sat down, making herself at home whilst Sophelia hesitantly followed suit.

"Who lives here?" She asked, worried about trespassing in someone's house.

"Rosemi." Teara replied nonchalantly.

"And she doesn't mind us being here?"

"No. She always said I'm allowed in here. And I'm allowed to bring someone I trust in here if I want. And I trust you."

"Thanks." Sophelia said touched. Teara was her best

friend, but such an outward sign of emotion from her was rare.

"Should we take a look at this paper then?" Teara asked, confused as to why Sophelia's eyes were looking a bit more teary than usual.

"OK what page was it?"

"Nineteen."

Teara got out the newspaper and turned it to page nineteen, laying the paper on the table, so they both could see it. When the two girls saw the headline, they gasped.

<Chapter 8>

America's Downfall.

Straight away, Teara and Sophelia started to read.

From Britain To America And Back Again.
The 'Dream Squad' returns.

Fifteen years ago the terrorist group known as the 'Dream Squad' left Britain, hoping to take over America. It didn't take long until life had returned to normal in Britain and the majority of people thought that peace would last forever. But they were wrong. News has reached the Wizard Weekly *from America. We are sad to bring you the news that the 'Dream Squad' have conquered, and now rule over, America. It is hard to believe that they have succeeded in America what they couldn't do in Britain. As most of you will remember, the 'Dream Squad', led by Philon Dream, had very strict plans to bring Britain into what they called the 'golden age'. Included in these plans were the ideas to imprison the Clans, (people who refused to use their hidden magic,) and mythical creatures. Their plans also included the imprisonment of those who had not proven that they had mastered their hidden magic by the age of five. In the fifteen years after these plans had been put into action, many people, Clans and children alike, disappeared. Only a few of these people have ever been recovered. The few that were, wouldn't speak about what they had gone through. All interrogators could get out of them was 'big building' and 'work must work'. Very few of these survivors are alive today, most dying of shock or exhaustion.*

Thousands of people have disappeared in America, none have been recovered. Some of America's population has fled to other countries. Those who fled here to Britain, are now making plans to leave upon hearing the news of the 'Dream Squads' return. They are urging us to do the same. Our connections in America have this to say; "The atmosphere over here is full of fear. Tension keeps building with the worry of what will happen next. A few of the 'Dream Squads' recruits have been stationed at every town and city to keep order. Adults, Clans, Magical creatures and children alike have been taken to a place or places unknown. Some Witches and Wizards have been put in isolation after protesting against the 'Dream Squads' plans, or helping those who were being taken."

Left in charge of America is one of Philon Dream's brothers, Marlinio Dream. The other four brothers have left with Philon for Britain. Philon and his 'Dream Squad' arrived in Britain this morning. Rumours have it that he is much stronger than when he left Britain in the first place. We also have information that Philon's brothers will leave Britain in a couple of weeks. Each heading for a different country in the hope of conquering it. You may think that this is good news, but again we are afraid to say that you are thinking wrong. As most of our readers will remember, Philon Dream is the most terrifying, roughest and most persistent of all the six Dream brothers. It was he who caused most of the trouble all those years ago. Very few of those people who were alive back then, and can remember those dark times, will ever forget the atmosphere of fear and hatred that hung over everyone and everything. Even Witches and Wizards here at the **Wizard Weekly** *can tell that something is going to happen.*

We have advice for all of our readers. If you feel the need to leave then please do so. No-one will stop you, except maybe a few of the 'Dream Squads' recruits. But if you want to stay in this beautiful country, then, again, please do so. Remember the closer we stand together, the less harm will come to us. We are one. Whether we are a Clan, Wiccan or Wizard. Whether we want to leave or don't. If we stick together, eventually, we will succeed.

This story was reported by Mark Toppins.

Teara looked up at Sophelia, watching her shocked eyes scanning the paper, waiting for her to finish. When Sophelia looked up from the *Wizard Weekly* the expression of shock on her face had increased, the exact same expression mirrored on Teara's face as well.

For a moment no-one spoke. All that could be heard was the trees swaying in the wind. There was no other sound, it seemed as if the whole forest stood in silence in the shock of this new found knowledge. Teara looked down and re-read the article, just to make sure she had understood, praying she has misread or that in some way she was wrong. Finally, once Teara had turned away from the paper and accepted that what she has read was in fact the truth, Sophelia, hesitantly, spoke.

"Which of the Dream brothers was your father again, Teara?"

"Philon. The worst of the six." Teara, quoted the article, answering very slowly, the shock not having yet settled.

Silence enveloped them again. Teara stood up and walked over to the small hole, halfway up the wall which was used as a window. She looked out. Not looking at anything in-particular, just scanning the world outside the hut. Her head was full of thoughts, which bumped into each other. In a matter of minutes she had learnt more of her heritage than years of questioning. Why hadn't Alfred or even Rosemi told her? The two people who were supposed to love and care for her the most and they had kept this from her. But wasn't that the thing? They has cared about her so had left her in ignorant bliss. But why let her find out like this? Her head was starting to hurt.

Sophelia stood up and, very slowly, walked over to Teara. She placed a slightly shaking hand on Teara's shoulder, showing her friend that she still cared for her, was still there for her, no matter what she had just learnt. Teara turned her head to look at Sophelia's hand. She then looked at Sophelia and gave her a small smile. She turned back and resumed her study of the view from the window, returning to her inner turmoil.

"Teara....Are you alright?" Sophelia asked tentatively.

"Yeah...I'll be fine...It's just...No one a W.W.A knew of my family. But now they will. And they'll probably think I'm like my dad." Teara gave a shaky laugh, *what if I am?* She added in her head, not daring to say it out loud.

Sophelia turned her round so they were face to face again.

"Yes most of them will, more than likely, make the connection. But if they even know you they'll know that you're not even half like your father. Or you're Uncles. You are kind, loving and lively." Sophelia smiled. "Now where is that Teara, the Teara I know? The Teara who believes in herself and stands up for what she believes in."

Teara gave a small laugh, "She's right here..."

"Yes she is. You know it's usually me that worries what other people think. It's usually you who's getting me out of fights and stopping arguments. Who cares who your father and uncles are? I most certainly don't."

Sophelia smiled as Teara laughed again, a bit happier as her spirits rose. Sophelia sure did know how to cheer a person up if they were feeling down, Teara thought. Then another thought came to her, one that sent her spirit plummeting again, she spoke it out loud.

"I didn't even know I had uncles. Alfred never told me."

The two girls stopped smiling. Sophelia led Teara back to the two chairs they had recently vacated and sat them both down.

"All Alfred told me was that my dad was part of the Dream Squad. And all I could find out about the Dream Squad was that they were a group of people who were very evil and did some extremely bad things. I didn't have a clue that I had uncles as well." Teara finished.

"Well Alfred must have had a good reason for not telling you. He usually shares everything with you. Shall we go and ask him about it?" Sophelia asked.

"Maybe tomorrow morning. I don't think I can face anymore earth moving revelations right now. We'll meet outside Alfred's office, early. We'll ask him then. I know it's a Saturday but do you think your mum will let you?" Teara asked.

"Yeah, she should. I usually come up here anyway." Sophelia replied.

Silence enveloped them again. Both Sophelia and Teara thinking their own thoughts.

"Do you think they'll come here? Your dad and uncles I mean." Sophelia asked.

"I don't know, they might. I guess we will just have to add it to the list of things to ask Alfred tomorrow." Teara answered in a voice of indifference.

Just then the door opened making Teara and Sophelia jump. Rosemi walked in.

"Hi girls." She greeted them.

"Hi Rosemi." The two girls replied.

"Sophelia, it's nice to see you again. But I'm afraid you will have to go home now as it is nearly night fall."

Rosemi told them.

"OK." Sophelia stood up, said good bye to Teara, giving her a quick and comforting hug, before walking out the door.

She walked over to a boy with short blond hair. He was wearing a t-shirt and shorts made out of linen. They both disappeared in a spiral of green leaves.

Rosemi shut the door and sat in Sophelia's vacated chair, raising her eyebrow in question of Teara's depressed expression. Without uttering a word, Teara pushed the newspaper towards her and Rosemi picked it up and began to read.

<Chapter 9>

Speak of the Devil

The next day arrived in bright sunshine, as if the sun was making a last attempt to shine before the inevitable winter began. Teara awoke beside the pond, having dozed off there the night before.

In a sudden rush all of the events from the previous day came rushing back to her. The Pure Heart Shield lesson. The talk with Alfred. The argument with Vinnie and the twins. The ride through the forest with Spirit and Sophelia. The article in the *Wizard Weekly*. The news of her father and uncles return to Britain. The talk with Rosemi by the pond.

All the thoughts, feelings and memories came back to her. Teara sat up and crossed her legs. Her father was back in Britain. The thought sent waves of curiosity, happiness and fear through her.

Teara was torn in two. She was happy that her father was alive and possibly only a couple of miles away from her. However she couldn't help being upset.

Why hadn't her father come to see her straight away? Why hadn't Alfred told her she had five uncles? What had happened to her mother?

All these questions and more were buzzing around in her head. She decided to ask Alfred each and every one of these questions when she saw him later on, and was determined to get answers.

Strangely enough, Teara was not angry at Alfred for not telling her anything about her father or what her father had done. Sophelia was right. And so was Rosemi. Alfred must have had a perfectly good reason to why he had not told her. He was sure to answer her questions when they both went to question him about it later.

Teara looked up at the sky where a flock of birds were passing throught the dew wispy clouds that lay dotted in the sky, the sunlight glancing off their wings. She got up and had a drink form the pond. Refreshed by the feeling of the cold liquid running down her throat, Teara looked over towards the huts which lay empty as the Nymphs who inhabited them had left earlier for their walk.

Rosemi had said last night that they were giving a ceremony to a baby nymph that had been born a couple of days ago. Teara had held that newborn Nymph to her chest, marveling in the complete trust the newborn baby held in her. It was a baby girl with a couple strands of pink hair coming out of her head.

Teara smiled at the thought. The ceremony must be the naming one, where the Nymph child is given a name and blessed by the chieftess Nymph. Teara would have preferred Rosemi to stay with her but seeing as Rosemi was the chieftess Nymph of this tribe, she was obligated to be there.

Teara looked at her clothes. She was still wearing her academy uniform. Through all the revelations of the night before she had forgotten to change. Teara stood up and snapped her fingers. Obediently her clothes changed. She was no longer wearing her academy uniform, but a pale blue top that had one sleeve reaching all the way down to her right wrist. She was also wearing a matching blue skirt that reached half way down her thigh. She had flip flops on her feet and her green necklace around her neck.

Teara walked over to the pond to look at her reflection.

"Perfect." She said. In a swirl of green leaves she disappeared.

***

At the outskirts of the forest, by the field, Teara reappeared in another spiral of green leaves. She looked down at her feet.

"Na, I think some dolly shoes would be better." She snapped her fingers again and her flip flops changed into a stylish pair of blue flats.

Teara started to walk towards the academy. She could see a couple of people here and there in the academy uniform. There were a few students who went Saturday school, most of whom were locals.

It wasn't long till Teara was following the familiar path across the field, passed the playground, up the stone steps, through the oak doors and into the academy. She walked up the staircase to the fourth floor and walked down the corridor that lay to her left. Her shoes clip-clopping on the floor and the sound echoing around her in the empty corridor. As Teara reached the end of the corridor, the familiar door of Alfred's personal office came into view.

Leaning against the wall, beside the door, was Sophelia. She was wearing a red tank top with white trousers and a red belt. She was also wearing high heels that were bright red, with little black bows on each ankle.

When Sophelia saw Teara coming she stopped fiddling with the old gold ring on her finger and stood up straight.

"Hey Soph, you alright?" Teara asked when she reached her.

"Yeah, as fine as can be considering the situation, you?" Sophelia replied.

"OK." Teara answered shortly, covering up how she really felt. Before she could change her mind she knocked on the door and a voice on the other side said,

"Come in."

Teara and Sophelia took a deep breath, preparing themselves, and walked in.

Alfred was sitting at his desk writing on what looked like reports. On seeing Teara and Sophelia he stored them in the top draw of his desk.

"Hi girls, come on in, sit down."

Teara and Sophelia returned his smile and sat in the two chairs in front of his desk.

"So girls, what can I do for you today?" Alfred asked.

"Well you remember the newspaper you gave to Teara yesterday?" Sophelia asked, once she realized Teara wasn't going to speak. Alfred nodded.

"Well we have some questions about it." Sophelia finished.

"Naturally. Ask away." Alfred said looking from Teara to Sophelia to Teara again.

"How come you never told me about what my father had done? Or about my uncles?" Teara asked quietly, her voice so soft it was barely a whisper.

"You were young. I didn't want you to know about it as it would have ruined your childhood. I didn't want you worrying about what your father had done and what he was about to do, no one needs to grow up with that on their shoulders. Whatever your family does or have done in the past shouldn't come to rest on you." Alfred replied.

Sophelia and Teara nodded in understanding. Teara knew she would not have liked knowing. She was OK with knowing now as she was old enough to know it wasn't her fault, although she had thought along those lines the night before.

"And for the same reason I didn't want you to know about you uncles." Alfred said. Teara nodded again.

"What are my uncle's names? The newspaper

mentioned one of them but I still don't know the rest." Teara asked.

"The six Dream brothers are; Philon Dream, Marlinio Dream, Alexando Dream, Jupitarni Dream, Thor Dream and Satárn Dream." Alfred said ticking them off. "Your dad was the third brother. Thor was first, Marlinio second, Alexando fourth, Satárn fifth and Jupitarni sixth. Out of all of them I only know of one offspring." Alfred said.

Teara looked up to find Sophelia and Alfred looking at her.

"Me." She said and Alfred nodded.

"Yes you." He said

"But what happened to Teara's mother?" Sophelia asked. Evidently, she had been thinking along the same lines as Teara.

Alfred looked at Sophelia. An expression of shock was written across his face but he smiled at her. Sophelia smiled back.

"I think it's time to tell you." Alfred sighed.

Both Teara and Sophelia looked at him with puzzled expressions.

Alfred opened the middle drawer of his desk, moved the green emerald, which he had used to call Rosemi all those years ago, to one side and took out an aged piece of paper. He carefully unfolded it and placed it on the table between the two girls.

The paper was yellowing and had obviously gotten wet a long time ago. The ink had ran in the past making the words hard to make out. Teara and Sophelia leaned forward to read it, after they finished they sat back in the same positions, each with a different picture, idea and view of Philon Dream in their heads.

Alfred took the note and carefully replaced it into the middle drawer. Shutting the drawer he looked solemnly up at the two friends.

"What you have just read," Alfred said, "Is the note that I found when I found Teara in that basket." He pointed to a basket made out of water reeds on one of the shelves in a corner. Where Teara had once laid now lived a bundle of fragrant herbs.

"So he killed my mum?" Teara asked, hoping against hope that the water damage had made her misread the writing.

"Yes." Alfred replied. Offering Teara no words of comfort, for there were no words to comfort someone when they find out that one of their parents killed the other.

Then Sophelia asked the question that Teara had been dying to ask since first seeing the note, but in light of what she had just been told, could not speak.

"Did you ever find the person that wrote that note?" Alfred shook his head.

"No. Rosemi and I looked for quite a few years, but we couldn't find them." Alfred said.

Silence enveloped them. Alfred not telling her was one thing, but Rosemi! Rosemi, whom Teara shared all her secrets with. Rosemi, the person that had been like a mother to Teara. Rosemi not telling her was another thing all together.

"Will he be coming here?" Sophelia asked.

"Who?" Alfred asked.

Teara was expecting Sophelia to be sarcastic, as she so often did when she felt a stupid question had been asked, but she wasn't. She probably knew this wasn't the time to be funny. Never the less, Sophelia's joking would have helped to lift the dark mood that had settled over the office. It would've added a bit of normalcy to the conversation.

"Teara's dad. Philon Dream." She said simply.

"He might, I don't know. I cannot begin to understand that man's motives and meanings he attaches to what he does or doesn't do." Alfred replied.

It was just as Alfred finished talking that a black flame suddenly appeared on Alfred's desk. Though most people would be scared the three just sat there, and patiently waited. The black flame burned in mid-air until as suddenly as it had appeared it disappeared.

However it left behind an envelope with Alfred's name written on it in an old fashioned calligraphy style. The envelope looked brand new and wasn't made of paper but of some old time posh linen. The flame hadn't caused it any damage because it was flame mail. The safest way to send a letter and impossible to intercept.

Alfred picked up the envelope and opened it. Inside was, of course, a letter. His eyes shot down to see who it was from.

"Speak of the devil and he will come." Alfred stated.

Teara and Sophelia looked at him in bewilderment.

"It's from your dad," He said simply and began to read the letter aloud.

"Dear Alfred Pine,

I hear you have been looking after my daughter during my absence. I will be arriving at your academy this afternoon, at promptly four o-clock. I will be coming by Pegasus. We will talk more thoroughly then. Please have my daughter, Teara, there as I am greatly looking forward to seeing her again. Thank you again and I look forward to seeing you this afternoon.

Philon Dream."

Once Alfred had finished, Sophelia spoke.

"He's coming here?" She asked trying to make sure she had understood.

"Yes," Alfred said.

"And he wants to see me?" Can Sophelia come too?" Teara asked, grasping her friends hand, she couldn't picture meeting this familiar stranger without the moral support that Sophelia would bring.

"I don't think she should." Alfred said apologetically. Sophelia opened her mouth to protest but Teara beat her to it.

"I'd feel much better if she did. After all she is pretty much a part of my family." The two girls smiled at each other, Sophelia comfortingly squeezing Teara's hand in gratitude. After a long pause of consideration, Alfred answered the two with a smile.

"OK,"

"Thanks," Sophelia said.

"Right, I suggest we all meet at the marble staircase by the front doors at three o-clock."

"OK," The two girls replied together.

"I will see you both at three then." Alfred said.

"See you at three," Teara said standing up.

"Bye," Sophelia said also standing up. The two girls walked out together, arms linked.

"Bye girls." Alfred said before turning himself to the preparations that would need to be made for Philon's impending visit.

<Chapter 10>

To Move or Stay.

For the remainder of the day Teara and Sophelia wandered around the grounds of the academy, spending time studying in the large library, eating lunch in the sunshine and playing pool in the rec room. Both of them becoming more excited and anxious as three o-clock drew nearer.

When three o-clock came Sophelia and Teara left the rec room, walked across the hall, and over to the main marble staircase to meet Alfred. It wasn't too long till Alfred came down the stairs towards them.

"Where are we going to talk to him?" Sophelia asked Alfred.

"I've set up a tea and biscuits set in one of the downstairs sitting rooms." Alfred answered. The three returned to silence, each lost in their own thoughts. Teara and Sophelia curious about what Philon would be like, Alfred trying to keep calm and civil, in light of someone he had fought hard against for years coming for a polite chat, it was increasingly hard to do so. The time passed until it was a quarter to four.

"Shall we go?" Alfred asked rhetorically. He started to walk towards the oak front doors, breathing deeply to keep himself calm. Sophelia followed and Teara took a deep breath before heading towards the door. Teara couldn't help but wonder what her father would be like. Would he know her as soon as he saw her? Or will he think she was just someone else? She had so many questions but no answers. The trio were now walking down the stone steps that lay in front of the academy.

"Mr. Pine..." Sophelia started.

"Please call me Alfred, Sophelia, Mr. Pine is for during academy time." Alfred interrupted.

"OK. Alfred, I've always wondered...why did you call this academy an academy and not a school? I mean an academy is a school funded by an outside source, but this place isn't." Sophelia asked and Teara smiled. Trust Sophelia to ask something that was completely off topic, although Teara had asked this question herself hundreds of times.

"Oh, because school sounds too old fashioned. Too much like the Clans." Alfred replied and all three of them laughed. The mood had suddenly lightened. Alfred pointed to the sky,

"There he is."

Teara and Sophelia looked up. In the distance a black dot had come into view in the otherwise clear blue sky. As the dot got closer, the trio could start to make out forms. The Pegasus was a beautiful dappling grey with a long mane. On its back was a man wearing a black suit with a matching cape on his back.

As the Pegasus got closer you could hear the steady flapping of its wings that pushed the air as it came in gracefully to land. Once the Pegasus had trotted to a halt, its rider hopped off as gracefully as his steed has landed.

"Thank you Pepper." The man addressed his Pegasus in a slight welsh accent. The man then walked over to where Teara, Sophelia and Alfred stood.

He had short black hair, in what Teara recognized as an old fashioned military cut, a pointed chin, a tanned face and grey eyes that looked pierced the soul of any who dared to look into them.

Teara didn't think he looked one bit fatherly. On the contrary he looked like a very intimidating businessman, someone who has come to negotiate a contract and nothing more. She couldn't help but compare the man in front of her with Alfred beside her.

"Alfred. Good to see you again." The man smiled. His smile was cold and didn't reach his eyes, it was a smile put on for a show, nothing more.

"Yes, you too Philon. I've heard of your success in America." Alfred said in a very cold voice, but Philon didn't seem to have noticed. He was now looking at Teara.

"And this must be my daughter Teara, am I correct?" Philon said.

"Yes," Teara replied with a small smile on her face.

"You look so much like your mother." Her father said, the smile was wiped off Teara's face as Philon moved onto Sophelia.

"And who is this beauty?" He asked, in a charming voice.

"This is Sophelia, my best friend," Teara introduced Sophelia, her voice held no emotion.

"Pleasure." Philon said and kissed Sophelia's hand making her blush bright red.

"Shall we go in?" Alfred asked, trying to gain control of the situation, as well as reminding Philon who was in charge.

"Yes, we shall." Philon said.

Alfred turned on his heels and started to walk up the stone steps. Philon followed him and soon the two men were in heated conversation.

Teara and Sophelia looked at each other before following the two men into the building. As they walked through the doors they saw Alfred waiting for them by a door to their right.

"Come on inside girls," He said, then disappeared into the room, the two girls following obediently.

They had entered a very attractive sitting room. There was two large brown, suede sofas, a matching armchair and an oak coffee table situated in-between the seats, all in the centre of the room. There was a cabinet with a tea set laid out on top of it. Plaques and awards that celebrated or congratulated the academy lined the walls, which were a calming cream colour.

Philon was sitting on one of the sofas and Alfred was in the armchair. They had each gotten themselves a cup of tea.

Teara and Sophelia walked over to the tea set. Sophelia got herself a cup of tea and Teara got herself a Mug of hot water and lemon. They then each took a biscuit and sat down beside each other on the empty sofa.

"So first of all, it's lovely to see you again Teara, and to meet your charming friend." Philon began, smiling at his daughter before turning on Alfred, "But Alfred, I'd like to know who has been looking after my daughter since she was taken from me. She seems healthy enough."

"Well she has been looked after and cared for by myself and the resident chieftess Nymph, Rosemi, whose tribe lives on the forest at the edge of the academy. I trust you have heard of Rosemi." Alfred informed him.

"Well who hasn't heard of Rosemi?" Philon replied, taking a drink from his cup. Meanwhile Sophelia gave Teara a look of shocked surprise.

"She is one of the five Nymphs who created the world after all." Philon finished.

"You never told me that." Sophelia said turning to Teara, as did everyone else in the room upon hearing Sophelia's outburst.

"It kinda...slipped my mind..." Teara replied apologetically.

"So let me get this straight. The Nymph that raised you just so happens to be one of the legendary five Nymphs that created the world we stand on, and it just slipped your mind to tell me." Sophelia said.

"Um...Yes..." Teara said smiling. Sophelia rolled her eyes before the two girls started to laugh. Alfred and Philon just looked at each other, both puzzled at the minds of teenage girls. Once the girls had calmed down, Philon started to move the conversation on.

"So, Rosemi has been looking after my daughter. That is most agreeable, much better than her being raised by a mere average witch. Has Teara got any unusual powers I should know about?" Philon asked, a look of greed slightly in his eyes.

"Well da." Sophelia stated before Alfred or Teara could speak.

"You can't expect Teara to grow up with the Nymphs and not pick up some powers." Sophelia said, shaking her head as if it was well known that Teara could use some Nymph powers.

"Well, the reason I have come is to ask Teara to come live with me." Philon said.

"To what...?" Teara and Sophelia said together.

"If you don't mind Philon, I would like Teara to stay here." Alfred said in a voice of ice.

"I don't think that's your decision." Philon said just as coldly, "I'm her father and I know what's best for her. You are merely someone who has been taking care of her during my absence."

"You've been out of her life for nearly thirteen years, I don't think you do." Alfred said standing up, his anger obvious in his glare.

"Don't you!?" Philon also stood up. The two men where now face to face.

"Actually," Sophelia started and the two men looked at her. "I think it's Teara's decision. She is nearly sixteen, she can decide what she wants for herself."

"Very well." Philon looked at his daughter expectantly.

"Teara. Where do you want to live?" Alfred asked, also turning his head to look at Teara.

Teara sat thinking. This wasn't a decision she could make in haste, even though she knew her heart told her to stay. She could go with her father and see all the evil he does and witness all the arrests he'd make. Or she could stay here. Where she felt calm, happy and at home. Where she had what was her real family and where she had always felt cared for, wanted and loved. It wasn't really a choice, in fact the more she thought about it the more she realized her heart was right, this was a decision she could make rashly.

"I want to stay here." Teara said quietly.

"I *beg* your pardon." Philon said, his anger palpable.

"I said I want to stay here. This place is my home. It always has been and it always will be." Teara said simply, shrugging her shoulders. If her father really cared about her, he would respect her decision. Unfortunately it looked like he didn't, as his anger seemed to radiate around him.

"Well I can see we are not going to agree." Philon said. He picked up his cloak and walked out. Alfred followed him. About five minutes later he returned into the sitting room.

"He's gone." He told them.

<Chapter 11>

Unexpected Assembly

Sunday came and went. Monday, Tuesday and Wednesday also passed. Soon Christmas had come and gone again and the seasons were leading into spring.

There had been no news on Philon, the Dream Squad or anything else, it was like they had disappeared from the face of the earth. It wasn't till the second Monday of spring that Teara, Sophelia or Alfred heard anything from or about Philon Dream.

It was morning. Teara was wearing her academy uniform, in preparation for a day of study. She was on the field in front of the forest, brushing down Spirit's coat, something that calmed her immensely, waiting for Sophelia. She would have been in the forest if it wasn't for Sophelia's fear of walking through it alone, and Teara hated to be the cause of her friend's discomfort.

Teara was just moving to brush down Spirit's mane when Sophelia ran over. She too was wearing her academy uniform, although today she had accessorized it with an orange scarf where a tie would've been.

Teara threw the brush up into the air and it disappeared into golden sparks. She then walked over to Sophelia.

"Hey Soph, What's the rush?" She asked smiling.

"Haven't...you...heard?" Sophelia panted.

"Heard what?"

"About your Dad and the Dream Squad?"

Teara stopped smiling.

"No I haven't." Teara said, she had been dreading this moment for months now, it was the reason she had been so on edge. So far no one has made had made the connection of Teara's heritage, or if they has they hadn't made a fuss about it.

"Well," Sophelia began, "Apparently the Dream Squad's started their recruiting process." She put her head to one side and continued. "Oh and something else that I can't really remember." Sophelia finished.

"What do you mean you can't remember?" Teara asked in desperation.

"I mean I can't remember, I've had two tests to study for, a long list of chores to do and a boatload of gossip to remember, excuse me if I wasn't listening properly and forgot something! But don't worry the school should be told of it anyway. Well that's what my mum says when she realized my mind had wandered." Sophelia replied.

She smiled at Teara apologetically and Teara smiled reassuringly back.

"Well, come on then Soph. If we don't hurry we're going to be late for Clan History."
"No! We can't be late. Come on Teara. We've got to go." Sophelia started to run full pelt towards the academy. Teara looked at her friend in amazement, no wonder her friend had been losing weight, with all this running it wasn't going to be long until she was an Olympic racer. She said a hasty goodbye to Spirit and ran after her, finally catching up at the stone steps.

"Hey Soph, stop. What's the hurry to get to lesson anyway?" Teara asked as Sophelia stopped. "Last I checked you hated Clan History."

"Well let me think." Sophelia said pulling a face like she was thinking hard. "Mmm. Well Calumeno moved into our class last week. But unfortunately, so did Vinnie, Wanda and Trix." Sophelia said.

"So?" Teara asked even though she had a feeling of what Sophelia was going to say.

"So, if we don't get there fast, we won't get seats next to Calumeno, and I may lose the one chance I have at winning his heart!" Sophelia said in desperation to get moving.

"Shoulda known this would have been about a boy. Here's an idea. Why don't I just shiver us up? Then we'll be there three times as faster." Teara said simply.

"That's a brilliant idea! Why didn't I think of that? Come on. Come on let's go." Sophelia rushed over to Teara and grabbed her hand, jumping up and down impatiently. Teara sighed and shivered them both up to Clan History, they were both encircled in small green leaves, the swirled faster and faster until all they could see were the green blur they created. Teara pictured the hall that was just outside the classroom they needed, it was then she felt the familiar leap of joy in her stomach. The small green leaves that had encircled them slowed until they started disappearing into the air. They both had reappeared beside an open door on the first floor of the academy. Sophelia immediately ran to look into the classroom.

"Teara, there's two seats next to Calumeno. Come on!" She disappeared into the classroom. Teara followed her. As she entered the classroom she could see Sophelia settling down next to Calumeno, already striking up a conversation.

Teara shook her head and walked over to where they were sitting. She put her bag beside the empty chair and sat down. Calumeno and Sophelia were already in deep conversation.

Teara took her pen and a piece of paper out of her bag and started to doodle. When she looked up she saw Vinnie and her crew coming in. Vinnie gave Sophelia a scowl of deep hatred, but Sophelia didn't notice. She was still too busy talking to Calumeno. Vinnie and her crew sat down on the other side of the classroom.

Teara carried on doodling. She was using a very special pen. When every child reached the age of two they are given a pen. This pen would never run out of ink and would only work for its owner. If the owner ever wanted to change the colour, they need only say the colour they wanted and the pen would obediently change to that colour. The same applied for when the owner wanted a pencil. The owner need only say pencil to the pen and it would change into one. If the owner ever lost the pen, all they needed to do was call it and it would appear in their hand. This method was very easy to use and the teachers loved it. Mainly because pupils could never make an excuse for forgetting their pen.

The class had turned silent. Teara looked up. At the front of the class was a man. He had short yellow hair, not blonde, bright yellow, and was wearing a neat black suit. On his right hand was a ring with a black rock on it. He was a Warlock. A type of Wizard who was born with the power of immortality. His name was Ceaser Downing, and he was there Clan History teacher.

"Right class. Today we are going to be learning about the Vikings. The Vikings were a society of people that..." Ceaser started but Teara's mind had already started to wander.

What was her Father up to? Why was her father recruiting? Teara was very happy that no-one had yet made the connection that she was related to the Dream Brothers. Teara prayed with all her might that there would be an assembly. She was sure that her brain would explode with all this curiosity and worry about her father.

"Teara." Sophelia hissed. Teara jerked back to reality.

"Yeah?" Teara answered.

"We've been given work and homework, Teara. And Mr. Downing's on the prowl, so if I were you I'd get started." Sophelia told Teara and handed her some plain paper.

"Um...Sophelia." Teara said.

"Uh huh." Sophelia said starting to write on her own paper.

"What are we meant to do?" Teara asked.

Calumeno leant over Sophelia to look Teara in playful shock

"Let me get this straight." He said. "Teara Dream wants help. Teara Dream, the smartest Witch in training in our class, is asking what to do."

"Yeah." Teara replied, surprised since Calumeno rarely talked to her.

"That's a first!" Calumeno said smiling.

"Well Calumeno, since you want to be such a smart Alek, why don't you tell me?" Teara replied also smiling.

Sophelia looked at them and shrugged. She mumbled something that sounded vaguely like 'boys' and carried on with her work. Her purple pen moving smoothly over the paper.

"Well Teara, since you asked so nicely, we have to write five hundred words on the Vikings." Calumeno told her.

"Five hundred words!" Teara exclaimed.

"Yes Teara, five hundred words." Calumeno's smile was broader than ever.

"That's a bit much isn't it?" Teara said, hoping it was a joke.

"Nope." Calumeno went back to his work. Teara took up her pen and started on the task she had been set, trying to remember anything and everything she had read or learnt on the Vikings.

Sophelia was already half way down her page. As much as Sophelia said she hated it, Clan History was her favourite subject. She just loved to know all about the Clans. Especially how they lived before the old Government realized that Nymphs were real.

Once the Government had realized and accepted this, the Nymphs started showing people that they had hidden magic, which was inside every one of them. There had been people who could use it before Nymphs has been discovered, but these people had been marginalized and ridiculed, labeled as freaks or psychics. Even some people today refused to believe in hidden magic. So much so that some of their children didn't even know it existed. These people lived in a few towns dotted around all over the world.

The end of the lesson was nearing and Teara was nearly finished her work. Sophelia and Calumeno were both in deep conversation again, seeing as they had both finished they're work earlier. Just as Teara was finishing her last sentence Mr. Downing started to talk.

"Right class. I want you to pack away. Your work on my desk please. Then I want to see you all back in your seats. Off you go." Mr. Downing very rarely used long sentences, preferring to be more quick and snappy. Getting to the point quickly with no description or elaboration.

The class followed his instructions, and once every one of them were back in his or hers seat, Mr. Downing continued.

"Now single file. By the door. I have to take you down to the hall. There is a very, very important assembly."

As the class lined up there was a lot of muttering and whispering. The class was still doing this by the time they had reached the hall. The tables where the students sat to eat their meals had been pushed to one side, and in their place was hundreds of chairs, facing the stage at the far end of the hall.

Teara managed to get a seat in between Sophelia and Calumeno, and in front of Brandon. The whole academy was soon in the hall. Nothing could be heard over the chatter that filled every nook and cranny of the large room.

A couple of minutes had passed when the pupils in the hall started to become quiet. Alfred walked into the stage and stopped when he hit the center point.

"Now. We have called you here to inform you of a very serious matter." Alfred begun. "Letters about this matter have already been dispatched to your parents via flame mail.

Some of you may have heard of the Dream Squad, and the crimes they had committed in Britain around fifteen years ago. Well for those of you who read the *Wizard Weekly*, you will know that the Dream Squad have returned."

The hall burst back into whispering and muttering. However these whispers and mutters were not full of the usual cheer that filled the academy. On the contrary these whispers and mutters were full of fear.

"May I have your attention please?" Alfred asked the assembly, which immediately became silent again.

"We have been informed that the Dream Squad have started their infamous recruiting process. There was a march yesterday to announce that, as they say, they are 'back in business'. There is news that the Dream Squad will be back to their old tricks by the end of the week.

Therefore, we are urging each and every one of you young Witches and Wizards, to continue going to your lessons. This means NO skiving." Alfred's eyes scanned the pupils.

"There is no need to worry. Nothing will happen to you while you are inside these walls. Now please, go to your lessons and carry on with your day." Alfred, after having dismissed the pupils, walked off stage and back to his office.

As the students were walking out of the hall to their lessons, their minds became full of questions and worries about the Dream Squad. The talk of the academy was sure to be about the assembly for a couple of days at least.

Teara and Sophelia were on their way to History. Except this time it was the history of Wiccans and Wizards and not of the Clans. Calumeno had left them to join up with some of his other friends.

Teara said goodbye to Sophelia, when they reached their classroom.

"Where are you going?" Sophelia asked.

"I need to be alone, I need a swim." Teara slung her bag over her shoulder and walked off.

<Chapter 12>

The Naturne.

Having left Sophelia and the others at their lesson, Teara shivered to the pond of *Tsaoil*. Once there, she snapped her fingers and her clothes immediately changed from her academy uniform to a dark green bikini.

Teara then slipped into the cool water of the pond, enjoying the feel of the water over her skin. She did a couple of lengths and then swam over to the steep bank on one side. It had just occurred to her she was being watched.

Teara looked around, trying to spot who was watching her. A movement from inside the trees caught her eye. She turned round and saw Rosemi walking out from the trees.

"Oh Rosemi. You startled me."

"Sorry dear. Do you mind if I join you?" Rosemi asked.

"No. Come on in." Teara replied. Rosemi snapped her fingers and her dress of autumn leaves was replaced by a chocolate brown swimsuit. She then slid into the water next to Teara.

"So, what's up?" Rosemi asked.

"Why would anything be up?" Teara acted surprised.

"Well swimming when you'd usually be in lessons, usually indicates that something is up." Rosemi replied.

Teara laid onto her back, floating on the water, looking up at the sky.

"Oh nothing. Just we've been told that the Dream Squad had started recruiting again."

"Yes I heard about that." Rosemi replied.

Teara swam back to the bank and smiled at Rosemi. She then did a back flip into the water, swam under the waterfall and back to Rosemi. When she got back she looked up, the exercise making her feel better already.

"It's Ivy." Rosemi said following Teara's gaze till her own eyes looked at the green haired Nymph. They waved to him and received a wave back.

Ivy then jumped into the air and turned into the most beautiful bird Teara had ever seen. His wings were made of what looked like dark green flames that burned brightly. His tale was the waves of the ocean, the colour a deep blue with the white tips of foam at the ends of them, the waves flowing out from his body to the tips of the tail. His body was made up of autumn leaves that reflected the sunlight. His long slender neck was made up of different types of flowers ranging from the common daisy to a rare black rose, his feet looked like old tree bark and his claws glistened like diamonds, his beak looked like it was made out of black onyx and his eyes, they looked like stars. It was like someone had taken the best bits of nature and pulled them together into this one magnificent being.

Teara gasped as the bird flew off through the trees and up into the sky, trailing behind it what looked like sparkles of moonlight.

"Hm. He must off shivered somewhere." Rosemi said then did a couple of lengths of the pond.

Teara was still staring at the spot where Ivy had changed into the bird. She couldn't understand why Rosemi hadn't seen it. Was this just more evidence of her weirdness? When Rosemi had finished swimming and had returned to where Teara was, Teara spoke.

"He didn't shiver Rosemi. Didn't you see it?"

"See what?" Rosemi's face was full of concern.

"Ivy turned into a bird. And a beautiful one at that." Teara said. Rosemi smiled. She had an idea of what

Teara had seen, but had to ask her one request to check that her suspicions were correct.

"Describe the bird to me, Teara." Rosemi smiled reassuringly.

Teara gave a sigh of relief. She had been worried that Rosemi would think that she was crazy. Teara described the bird to Rosemi, still unsure on whether Rosemi thought she was crazy or not.

After she had finished talking there was a pause between them while Rosemi thought of how to phrase her answer. The only sound was those of nature, which was all around them.

"Teara. I think you saw Ivy turning into a Naturne. I didn't know we had one in this tribe, but that only proves that I don't know this tribe as well as I thought." Rosemi smiled.

"I saw a what?" Teara asked.

"A Naturne." Rosemi replied simply.

"What's a Nature?" Teara asked and Rosemi laughed.

"Naturne not nature. I keep forgetting, Teara, that you're not a proper Nymph. A Naturne is a bird created by nature to protect it. They are very rare, and can only be seen if they allow you to see them." Rosemi told her.

"Then why could I see it?" Teara asked.

"There is only one reason Teara, unless the Naturne shows itself to you, you cannot see it. That is unless you too are a Naturne." Rosemi said.

"Are you saying I'm a Naturne!?"

"Yes. Thought I won't say I'm surprised. Naturnes are usually creatures who spend their time close to nature, protecting and nurturing it. There have been many human ones, though they are usually Nymphs because of a Nymphs direct connection to nature. I believe there was even a vampyre one once."

"But you're a Nymph and you're not one." Teara

pointed out and Rosemi laughed again.

"Yes Teara. I'm not a Naturne. Not all Nymphs are. That is why I didn't see what you saw. If everyone who was connected to nature was one there would be too much conflict. Having Naturnes few and far between leaves nature to be cared for in a more direct way. The person can focus on what is needed and not with arguing about the direction they should take with another."

"Oh I understand. So when will I be able to change into one like Ivy did?" Teara asked, her previous depression gone replaced by growing excitement.

"It changes with every being. You see Teara. The Naturne was created to keep nature alive." Rosemi replied.

"But I thought that's what Nymphs are for."

"Yes it is also a Nymphs job. And that is why a Naturne is usually a Nymph, you see the two do practically go hand in hand. The power that being has is great, another reason why there is so few."

"So I won't have that much power." Teara said, trying to keep that she was upset from Rosemi.

"You'll be more powerful than the average Wizard or Witch. There's this legend Teara. That one day a Naturne will have a terrible duty. That duty will be to protect the Earth.

You see a great evil will come in the form of a Nymph. This evil will want the Earth for its own. All the Naturnes and Nymphs of the world will direct all their power to that one Naturne. That Naturne and the Evil will fight and the winner will take the Earth.

If the Naturne won then the Earth will return to normal. But if the Evil won, the Earth would be thrown into unspeakable darkness." Rosemi concluded.

"Unspeakable darkness is bad right?" Teara asked and received a friendly punch in the arm and laugh from Rosemi.

"OK, OK. I know it's bad. Does the legend say when this will happen?" Teara asked.

"Oh not in your lifetime, I wouldn't think. The legend has been around for millennia and I'm sure it will continue to be around for many more. OK Teara, I think it was time you got back to lesson. Don't you think?" Rosemi said.

"Yes." Teara laughed. She hopped out of the pool and snapped her fingers. She was again dry and wearing her academy uniform. Teara couldn't wait to tell Sophelia what had happened.

"Bye Rosemi." Teara said as she shivered back to the academy, just in time for her next lesson.

Rosemi smiled and shook her head. Teara was a very strange child, she thought, and one with a lot of pressure resting on her shoulders. She just hoped she wouldn't crumple from that pressure. Rosemi ducked under the water and carried on swimming, returning her thoughts to the clearing that she loved.

<Chapter 13>

An Encounter with Love

The next day came in a fresh breeze, a bright sun and a sparkling dew. Spring was nearly over and summer was on its way. Teara had yet again spent the night in the forest, except this time she had slept in a clearing with the unicorns, curled up among dome moss against a boulder.

The unicorns must have left whilst she slept as Teara awoke with nothing but the forest around her. She lay there for a while under the trees, staring up into their branches. The sky was almost invisible to her as she was too deep in the forest and the trees blocked out so much sunlight that only a few rays managed to pierce to the clearing below.

A squirrel came down from a tree to get a nut. Teara was soon chattering away to it in squirrel tongue. This was not unnatural for anyone who had spent their lives watching nature interact. Living in the forest had enabled Teara to learn how to speak in almost each of the creatures own language. Where most of her peers could converse in many of languages of many countries, Teara had never been able to master another human tongue, but the languages of the animals came easily to her. At the moment she was learning how to speak zebra from one of the Nymphs.

After the squirrel and Teara had finished their conversation, the squirrel left to enjoy his nut and Teara returned to looking at the tree branches again. This was one of her favorite past times. Staring up into the sky or branches, and admiring the nature around her, random thoughts creeping into her head.

She hadn't told Sophelia about the talk with Rosemi

or about the Naturne yet, as she wasn't ready to answer the barrage of questions that were sure to be asked. Teara decided she'd tell Sophelia later on today. One of the Nymphs, Thorn, was bringing Sophelia into the forest around lunchtime. She'd tell her then.

Teara had a soft spot for Thorn. He was a very handsome Nymph with dark blue hair and deep green eyes, needless to say it was the colour of his hair that had led to blue becoming her favourite colour.

The only problem was, they both went shy around each other. Which was very unusual for Thorn, for whenever he was around everyone else he seemed to be very talkative.

Thorn was the only a year older than Teara and just a little bit taller than her. Little did Teara know that Thorn had exactly the same feelings for her as she had for him, but each of them couldn't bring themselves to tell the other of their feelings.

Teara lay there for over an hour just thinking of random stuff, until her mid went blank and she relaxed into a calm, peaceful state. The gentle breeze playing through the blond strands of her hair.

When half twelve had arrived Teara sighed. She'd have to make a move to meet Sophelia at the Pond of *Tsaoil*. She had been delaying it for a while.

Teara stood up and shivered to the clearing. A couple of small Nymphs were playing in the cave behind the waterfall, throwing an acorn to one another. Other than that the place was barren of any over living creatures. Clearly Thorn and Sophelia were not here yet.

Teara went and sat on a rock that lay at the edge of a clearing. She had to unhook her Nymph dress as it had snared itself on a jagged piece of the rock.

Part of Teara couldn't wait for Sophelia to arrive as she really wanted to see Thorn. Then again, the other part of Teara was dreading the moment when Sophelia arrived. Teara hated going shy as she hated not being in control of the situation, and being shy left her all flustered.

A light laugh broke the silence of the clearing. Teara looked up. There, on the other side of the clearing, was Sophelia and the handsome Thorn.

Teara thought she recognized that laugh. It was the laugh Sophelia gave when she was either flirting or with an incredibly cute guy and Teara felt a flash of anger at her friend for flirting with him. However, Sophelia knew how Teara felt about Thorn so would never ask him out. Though, in Sophelia's book, that didn't mean that she wasn't allowed to flirt with him.

Teara stood up and walked over to Sophelia and Thorn.

"Hi Teara." Sophelia said.

"Hi Soph." Teara answered. Her voice was timid and a bit quieter than usual.

The two girls gave each other a friendly hug. Both of them then turned to look at Thorn.

"Hi T-Teara." Thorn said.

"Hi Thorn." Teara replied quietly. Teara's stomach felt as if it was full to the brim with butterflies that just wouldn't stay still.

Sophelia gave Teara a little push towards Thorn. Teara looked back at her. Sophelia's expression couldn't have been clearer. Talk to him. That's what her expression was saying for her to do, she just didn't think she could.

Teara faced Thorn again. When she spoke she chose her words carefully so as not to make a fool out of herself.

"How...are you...Thorn?" She asked timidly.

"Um...Fine thanks...you?" Thorn answered just as timidly as Teara. He too was choosing his words carefully.

"OK..."

There was a pause where no one spoke.

"Well, I guess we will see you later Thorn." Sophelia said. It was clear to her that this conversation was going nowhere fast. These two were clearly not going to make any more progress in their relationship today.

"Oh. OK. Goodbye Sophelia. G-Goodbye Teara." Thorn said and without giving Teara time to say goodbye, he disappeared in a spiral of red leaves.

Teara stood staring at where Thorn had last been. Sophelia walked over and sat down on the rock that Teara had recently vacated.

"So Teara. What's up?" Sophelia said. Teara didn't answer. She just stood there staring at the same spot.

"Teara...Teara...TEARA!!!" Sophelia shouted. Some birds flew out of a nearby tree. Teara jerked back to reality like she'd just been woken from a deep sleep.

"Yes Sophelia. Did you say something?" Teara asked as she walked over and sat on the ground next to her friend.

"I asked what's up with you. You walked away from history without going to class, and then reappeared an hour later full of smiles. Now I want to know what caused the change or are you just becoming a megalomaniac?" Sophelia said with a menacing smile plastered on her face.

"Are we bringing out the long words now? And yeah, I forgot to tell you." Teara replied. She then told Sophelia all about seeing Ivy turning into the beautiful bird, which she had later found out was a Naturne. She told Sophelia about the legend. How Rosemi had told her all about the Naturnes. Teara finally concluded her story by telling Sophelia about how Rosemi said that she too was a Naturne.

Sophelia sat in silence and listened to the very end. When Teara had finished, Sophelia spoke.

"So let me see if I got this straight. You see a Naturine-thingy..."

"Naturne." Teara corrected her.

"Right, one of those. You see a Naturine and all of a sudden you have this power to turn into one of the, what you call, most beautiful creatures in the world." Sophelia looked at Teara with an expression of wonder and amazement.

"Pretty much. Except I haven't got my powers yet." Teara answered. A big grin spread across Sophelia's face.

"When?" She said.

"When what?" Teara said not understanding the question.

"When do you get your powers?" Sophelia said, excitement coming out of her from every direction.

"I don't know. Rosemi said it changes with everyone. Though she did tell me last night that the most common age is sixteen. It was when the witches of old were said to come of age." Teara answered.

"But it's your sixteenth birthday in a fortnight. That's only two weeks!" Sophelia stated.

"Oh yeah. I forgot about that." Teara replied.

"Wait a minute. That legend said a Naturne would one day have to save the world. That Naturne could be you!"

"I doubt it. Rosemi said it probably wouldn't happen in our lifetime."

"Oh." Sophelia's smile fell. "But Rosemi's a Nymph. She can't die unless she's stabbed in the heart with a titanium dagger or wishes to die with every ounce of her body and soul. Can't she?"

"Yes that's true. But I meant in our lifetime you dufus." Teara and Sophelia laughed.

"Oh yeah, Soph. I got a flame mail from Alfred this morning." Teara said.

"Alfred Pine?" Sophelia asked.

"How many Alfred's do we know?"

"Five actually." Sophelia said and Teara shook her head.

"Yes, Alfred Pine. He wanted to know if he could see me. He also said you can come to as, according to him, we are practically inseparable." They laughed again.

"Come on then. We can stop in the library on the way. I want to pick up *Myths and Legends; which is true and which is false.* To find out more on this Naturine stuff." Sophelia said standing up.

"OK. And it's Naturne." Teara stood up. "Wait a second. Let's take Spirit and Satin." Teara whistled. A couple seconds later Spirit appeared and behind him was a beautiful unicorn. Its coat was white with a hint of lilac and on its forehead was a horn the colour of lilac and formed in a perfect spiral, just like Spirits.

Teara walked over and hopped onto Spirit's back. Sophelia jumped onto Satin with an exclamation of,

"She's beautiful, I love her coat." and then they both rode off into the deep forest.

<Chapter 14>

The Whisper.

Having reached the end of the forest, Teara and Sophelia dismounted from their unicorns. They said thank you for the ride and watched the two unicorns gallop off into the forest, playing with one another as they did.

Teara and Sophelia had just reached the stone steps when they heard a snide voice.

"Oh look who it is."

With a sigh, Teara and Sophelia turned around. Standing in front of them was Vinnie Stocksworthy and her crew of copycats; the twins, Wanda and Trix, and two other girls. One of the girls had short spiky hair, a nose piercing and was wearing a choker, whilst the other had brown tied back into a ponytail. Each and every one of them was scowling at Sophelia.

"And what do you two think you're doing?" Vinnie asked.

"Well last time I checked it was none of your business!" Sophelia snapped, her short temper rising.

"Shouldn't you geeks be in lesson?" Trix sniped and the short haired girl made a sound somewhere between a snort and a laugh.

"Well, no. Our year has this lesson off. It's called a free period." Teara replied simply.

"And were we talking to you? Go tear-a piece of fashion out of a magazine or something. It'll be much better than that rag." Wanda snarled.

"Oh good one Wand." the brown haired girl and Wanda gave each other hi-fives, as if they had just run a 10 mile marathon, and not simply mixed a few words together to form an insult.

Teara looked down at her Nymph dress. Nymph clothes were always in the style as the nymphs never changed style, if something was functional then they would keep it until it no longer was. It saved time, energy and material, but thinking on it, Teara decided it wasn't really right for lessons. Especially as everyone else, including Sophelia, was wearing the school uniform.

Teara snapped her fingers and her clothes changed in to a stylish, sleeveless black top, with the school insignia blazoned across her chest, and twentieth century jeans. Black calf high boots appearing on her bare feet.

"Cool!" The spiky haired girl said but soon was staring at her feet from all the dirty looks her friends gave her. Teara smiled.

"Think you can show off with those stupid powers of yours? You're just a freak, someone who no one wants around, someone..." Vinnie started but Sophelia interrupted her.

"Oh shut up Vinnie. You're just jealous."

Vinnie ignored Sophelia's comment and turned her anger on her instead.

"You can shut your trap hole as well *Ginge*. Everyone knows you're a boy stealer now."

"And why am I a boy stealer? And isn't that word like a hundred years old or something?" Sophelia asked, her voice cold.

"Why? Isn't it obvious enough for you? You stole Calumeno. When everyone knows he's mine. Everyone can see we are meant to be." Vinnie flicked her hair.

"Well he clearly can't see it! He didn't exactly say he was saving those seats for anyone, least of all you, Vinnie. He didn't tell me to leave, or to not talk to him. No one can steal a person. As, in case your too thick to notice, people chose what they want to do. Nobody can choose for them. That's part of the free will thing we've got going on." Sophelia said.

"Liar!" Vinnie snapped," Why would Calumeno have you..."

"When he can have Vinnie Stocksworthy?" Trix finished.

"And worthy of the stocks she is." Teara stated calmly.

Vinnie looked taken aback. Of all the time she had known Teara, Teara had never sniped back. Even if it was in that annoyingly calm voice of hers.

"Why would Calumeno go out with that Ginge?" Wanda said.

"Wanda. You, Vinnie, and all the rest of you are just such hypocrites." Teara said shaking her head, growing impatient with this childish talk.

"And just why are we hypocrites?" Trix snapped, angry at Teara.

"Well isn't it just so obvious to see. All of you talk about having the latest stuff. You put people down if they don't use the latest slang, yet you all still use insults like Ginge, Geek and Boff. I mean those insults are from the Twenty-first century. Look at your calendars. That's ages ago. Don't you think it was about time some new nicknames were invented?" Teara said. "Come on Sophelia."

Teara pulled Sophelia up the stone steps, leaving Vinnie and her crew below looking slightly abashed. As they were walking through the oak doors they heard Vinnie's voice shout up to them.

"Stay away from Calumeno!"

Once Teara and Sophelia were inside the academy they burst out laughing, making them get some very strange looks from passing students.

"Problems. That girl has some major problems." Teara told her friend.

As they walked to the library, which was right at the back of the academy on the ground floor, they chatted about what had happened, discussing just how troublesome Vinnie's problems must be for her to act so rotten.

Once they reached the library, Sophelia went down one of the curved aisles to find the book she was looking for. Teara waited by the door, admiring the sparse size of the room.

The library was a huge round room. The walls were covered in shelves that full to the brim of books. The aisles were designed to curve like the walls, so it was like a gigantic round maze. More than once Teara and Sophelia had managed to get themselves lost in here, looking for a book but not having a clue where to start. In the middle of the room was a space where people could sit and read. This space had the checkout desk at one end. The rest of the space was filled with bean bags, tables and chairs that lay scattered around.

Whatever book you wanted, this library was sure to have it, just finding it was going to be the problem. Teara didn't think even the librarian knew where all the books were, but she couldn't blame them, there was only so many books one person could recall.

Soon Sophelia reappeared from behind one of the aisles.

"Shall we get going then?" She said tucking the brown leather bound book into her bag.

Teara nodded and they set off for Alfred's office. The pictures on the walls blurring by, as they walked. Pretty soon they were there. Teara knocked and Alfred's familiar voice came through the door.

"Come in."

Teara and Sophelia walked in to the now all too familiar office. Alfred nodded to them then nodded his head to the two seats in front of his desk.

The two girls sat down in the seats that he had indicated as Alfred put down his own special pen and looked at them. Teara had a funny feeling they were about to be told something bad. And she didn't need any more bad in her life, if anything she needed a big wallop of good news.

"Well I'm sure you two are aware..." Alfred started and Teara took a sharp intake of breath. This *was* going to be bad, she knew it. Was it going to be about her Father? Or her uncles? Or had Alfred found something even more horrible to tell her? Did she have a grandmother who sucked the blood of children? Ok now she was just being crazy. She halted her runaway thoughts as Alfred continued.

"...That it is Teara's birthday in only two weeks' time." Teara let out her breath. Whatever she had expected, it wasn't this. Alfred smiled at the two girls.

"So Teara. What type of party would you like to have?" he asked.

"P...P...Party!?" Teara stammered. Still trying to get her head round the fact that she wasn't going to be told something heart wrenching, life threatening or world ending. That what Alfred wanted was to talk about something so trivial as her birthday, something she didn't really care for.

"Yes Teara, a party. For your birthday." Sophelia said bringing Teara back down to earth. Sophelia had evidently known about this all along, Teara thought. Sure enough, both Alfred and Sophelia, had giant grins on their faces.

"Oh. Um. How about a tea in the forest?" Teara replied. Trying to keep things simple and the prices down. The grin slowly slid off Alfred's face.

"Oh well...just a dinner...and in the forest. Why in the forest Teara? That can't possibly be safe. I mean..." As Alfred broke into a lecture about how dangerous the forest was, something distracted Teara. She looked over to the open window.

"Teara..." There it was again. A voice, barely above a whisper, calling her name.

"Did you hear that?" Teara asked Alfred and Sophelia. Alfred looked at Teara in a weird expression. Teara wasn't sure if he was annoyed with her for interrupting him, or whether something else was wrong.

"Hear what?" Sophelia asked timidly.

"Teara..." Came the whisper.

"That!" Teara said impatiently and Sophelia shook her head.

"We can't hear anything Teara. There's nothing there." Sophelia said.

"Teara are you alright?" Alfred asked, concerned that she was coming down with a cold.

"Yes, yes. I'm fine. It was nothing. Just my mind playing tricks on me." Teara reassured them. The last thing she needed was for Alfred to think she was ill, it would just add more ammunition to his argument that the forest wasn't good for her health. She'd look into this mysterious whisper later, as she was sure she wasn't imagining it, her imagination couldn't be that overactive.

"What were you saying Alfred?" Teara asked. Trying to move the conversation on and away from the whisper.

"I was just saying that I don't like the idea of a meal in the forest." Alfred sighed, "But if that is what you want, I'm sure it can be arranged." Teara nodded.

"Thank you," She said, "We'll be seeing you later then." Teara and Sophelia got up and walked to the door. As Teara was about to open it, Alfred called them back. He handed Teara a newspaper. Alfred and Teara nodded to each other. Inside this paper must be the bad news she was expecting, she didn't think Alfred would have called her up here to simply find out what she wanted to do for her birthday.

Teara walked over to Sophelia, and they both exited the office. Teara was determined that Sophelia and she would read the paper away from prying eyes.

<Chapter 15>

More Trouble

Once Teara and Sophelia had reached the bottom of the steps, Sophelia spoke.

"Which paper is it this time? We know the *Wizard Weekly* has been reporting on everything that has been happening...but we don't know if the other papers have been saying the same."

Teara had been wondering the same thing. Oh well, great minds think alike, she thought. Teara opened the paper to the front page. As she did she realized why Alfred had not told her a pacific page to look at, there was no need. It was hard not to notice the big, bold letters that made up the headline.

Mass Kidnapping!!! Were the words emblazoned across the page. Sophelia noticed Teara's expression immediately.

"T...Teara? Is it bad?"

Teara's eyes were just staring at the same spot, her mind going into shock. Sophelia's voice seemed distant, like it was on another planet. She knew something like this was coming, she just didn't expect the disgust, worry and shame that came with it. Shame that she was a blood relation of the man that had done this, disgust that someone she was related to would do this and worry. Worry that her life was about to change, once her peers knew of her heritage there was no guarantee that they would treat her the same.

Sophelia was starting to get worried. Teara had gone deathly pale. It took a while but eventually Teara answered her and relief flooded through her.

"It's the *Daily Witch*. And look at the front page." Teara held up the paper for Sophelia to see. This time it was Sophelia's turn to go pale.

"Come on." Sophelia said and, not unkindly but still urgently, started to pull Teara towards the oak doors. 'Who cares about next lesson, this is more important' Sophelia thought. She had to get Teara somewhere quiet and private. Not the forest as that was sure to be full of Teara's friends.

The two girls were now at the bottom of the stone steps. Sophelia continued to pull Teara around one side of the academy. They went over to the small shack that lay about fifteen meters in front of them.

Squawks, squeaks and all kinds of noises were coming from inside the shack. This was were some of the permanent pupils kept their pets. There was a mixture of rats, lizards, hamsters and even a parrot or two. Once they were behind the shack and had double checked that no one could see them, they opened the paper.

After the headline the paper said the full article could be found on page three of the newspaper. As fast as Teara could, she turned to page three, her hands shaking, barely able to keep the paper steady, and the two girls started to read.

Mothers Weep for Their Lost Children!!!

Yesterday the 'Dream Squad' made their latest movement in aid of their cause, 'A Perfect World' otherwise known as 'The Golden Age'. In Inverness, a once magnificent city situated in Scotland, a mass kidnapping has taken place. The kidnapping took place at the Magical Ocean Academy (M.O.A.) A school that not only took local students but those from around the country that has showed an special ability with the ocean and marine life. The 'Dream Squad' are reported to have entered the building around five o clock as staff and students were having their evening dinner. Once in, Philon Dream placed a Death Chain around the staff. His recruits barricaded the students inside the hall and put them through a series of 'tests'. The ones that did not pass these tests were forcefully taken away. Some of the students fought against the 'Dream Squad' but to no avail. Around five hundred and twenty six students and two staff members were taken. One student, four parents and three staff members died in this tragic event each one were said to be trying to help the students. Emergency Wizards have no leads as to where the kidnapped children and staff are. Some of the other local schools have closed on the off chance that they are hit next, stating it would be harder for any more mass kidnappings to occur if there wasn't a place where students could meet in large numbers. Around one thousand people have already left Britain and there is sure to be lots more joining them. This kidnapping has only confirmed Emergency Wizard's fears. If the 'Dream Squad' continue killing and kidnapping, Britain will soon be in the state that it was in less than two decades ago. Emergency Wizards are asking anyone with any information whatsoever to contact them. The same applies for anyone with worries or concerns. We will try and keep you posted with the latest news. Keep safe. And remember when things don't turn out the way you planned, figure out a way to turn things around. This article was written by Michelle Chapolini.

Teara and Sophelia looked at each other. The look of shock not as big as they had expected. They had been told by several people that Philon was capable of more than this, but actually hearing about it was a different matter.

"Well. What do you think of it?" Teara asked, hiding all of her emotions on the surface but inside was a swirling storm of emotions.

"Um...Well...I suppose I'm a tad scared to be honest...I mean...Do you think he'll come here? To the Academy?" Sophelia asked.

"I don't know. Apparently he wants all Wizards and Witches who can't use their hidden magic taken away, as well as magical creatures. And the mythical ones." There was a pause until Teara spoke.

"And I won't let him."

"What?!" Sophelia asked looking at Teara.

"I won't let him. It says here..." Teara held up the newspaper.

"That he attacked the Magical Ocean Academy. Remember Carlita?"

Sophelia nodded. Carlita completed their old circle of friends but she had moved up country.

"Carlita goes there!" Teara said to Sophelia's shock and dismay.

"Carlita goes there and I haven't heard from her! The *Wizard Weekly* said the people recovered only spoke of 'work'. So I know that she is still alive. But now it's personal. Plus he wants to take away the ones I have grown up with. Magical and mythical creatures. The ones that I care about, that I love. That includes Spirit, Satin and his whole herd."

"But what can you do?" Sophelia asked, a bit scared at how much feeling was coming through in Teara's voice.

"I'm going to fight him. All of them. I won't let them win. I'm going to take the next couple of weeks to research all I can about my father. No. About Philon. He hasn't earned the right to be called father. I'm going to find out everything I can, I won't let my family be hurt. And I'm going to find out about Carlita. If I can't go up to Inverness myself I'll ask one of the nymphs to go. I have to find out if she is ok."

"Then I'm going with you." Sophelia said.

"No. No. You can't. I won't risk losing you." Teara looked at her best friend. When she was young it was only Sophelia and Carlita who had been there for her. They were the only ones her age she loved as deeply as Alfred and Rosemi. They were like sisters to her. It was hard enough when Carlita had moved away three years ago, but she'd had Sophelia to help her through it, and now Carlita may have been kidnapped by Philon. Teara didn't know what she would do if she lost Sophelia as well.

"I'm going. I can't let you do this alone. What kind of friend would I be then?"

"O.K." Teara nodded, reluctantly, knowing if she argued now, Sophelia would dig her heels in and she would get nowhere.

"O.K. Remember, we're in this together." The two girls gave each other a big hug. The forgotten paper falling silently to the ground.

"Come on. Let's get some dinner." Sophelia said.

"O.K." Teara and Sophelia walked back to the main building of the Academy. They went into the cafeteria and settled down to roast Duck, potatoes and various vegetables accompanied by a melon juice. Both trying their best to act normal and not notice the dark atmosphere they seemed to be carrying around with them.

***

Meanwhile back at the wooden shack, Vinnie and her crew were picking up the forgotten paper, which Teara and Sophelia had left behind.

Vinnie had spotted the two girls sneaking off somewhere and had decided to follow them. They had heard their whole conversation.

Vinnie's eyes skimmed the article. So this was what they were talking.

"So Teara Dream's dear old daddy's the leader of the 'Dream Squad'. And she has five uncles in it as well. That sounds like a family business if I've ever heard of one." Vinnie said slyly.

"Well, no wonder she's always acting like she's queen of everything. Now I wonder how she'd feel if this just so happened to get out. Girls, do you feel up to some rumour mongering?"

Vinnie's crew answered her with loads of 'Yeah', 'Of Course' and 'Well da'.

"Well, let's get to work then." Vinnie said pocketing the paper and leading her crew back to the academy, a large smirk plastered on her face. This may be exactly what she needed to break the popular view of Teara being a miss goody-goody two shoes. And what she needed to sway Calumeno's heart in her direction.

<Chapter 16>

Surprises

Two weeks passed and, as Teara vowed, she spent every free hour researching the 'Dream Squad', her family's crime group. Most of the stuff that she found just confirmed that most of the people the 'Dream Squad' had taken were never found again. Most of it wasn't very clear and seeing as it was classed as recent history, a lot wasn't recorded. However, Teara did find one book which proved that her worse fears were yet to come.

Though the Mass Kidnapping seemed terribly horrific, it was just the beginning. If it was anything like it was last time there would be mass murders next. Teara had asked permission to go and seek news of Carlita, but was denied, instead being told she wasn't to leave the academy campus or the cover or the forest. Rosemi did send Ivy to gather as much information as he could, but he returned only to say that Carlita had fought against one of her friends being taken, and thus had been taken among the others to an unknown place.

Teara had reached a dead end, all she could do was wait until she had any more information. She had read in the past that people used to pray to a higher deity for guidance or help. Teara didn't believe in anything of the like but she prayed anyway. Anything she could do to help her friend she would and if that meant praying to someone she didn't believe in and couldn't see, she would do it.

To keep Sophelia happy Teara didn't do any research the few days before her birthday, though she kept asking if they could forget about her birthday, she didn't feel like celebrating something as trivial as a birthday when it felt as if the world was collapsing around her. When she told Rosemi this, Rosemi imparted this piece of information to her;

'If we stop living and enjoying those most trivial moments that make our lives a happy place, then surely those who wish to bring darkness to our lives have already won?'

Teara knew there was some truth to what Rosemi said, but knowing it was true didn't stop her heart telling her that she was wrong. That she was betraying the friendship she had with Carlita if she continued living while she might die. But Teara ignored her heart and did as she was told, trying her very best to enjoy the few days that led to the date of her birth.

It wasn't long till her birthday arrived. Teara was going school as it was a Friday and the only lesson she had was Power Studies which was one of her favourites. She had been avoiding school since that day she had read the newspaper, making excuses to Rosemi and Alfred and spending her days huddled up in the library researching. But the few days she hadn't been researching she had grown bored and decided that she should return to lessons. If she missed much more she would fall behind.

Teara met Sophelia at the wooden sign which lay at the bottom of the stone steps. They greeted each other with their usual hug.

"Happy Birthday Teara!" Sophelia said. "I'll give you your prezzie tonight at dinner." Teara sighed mentally, at least one of them was happy and excited.

"O.K." Teara replied, forcing a smile to her face.

"Wow. Sixteen. A proper teenager now. That's something. Just means that you have to come to all of your lessons now." Teara gave Sophelia a friendly punch. "Have to be more responsible now and set an example to all of us younger ones." Teara raised her eyebrow at Sophelia in disbelief.

"O.K. O.K" Sophelia said laughing. "I know that will never happen, you're just too much of a lost cause. Come on. Let's get to lesson."

They walked up the stone steps and up the staircase to their classroom. As they went, Teara noticed something. As she passed her fellow students they broke out in whispers, which silenced as she came within hearing distance.

What was going on? Was there a surprise birthday party for her? Or was there something else going on? Or was she just being her usual pessimistic self?

When the two girls reached the classroom they took their usual seats. Seeing as there was still ten minutes to go till the end of the lesson, they decided to chat. In the middle of their conversation Vinnie and the twins walked over to them.

"What do you want?" Sophelia asked trying to keep her cool.

"Oh, we just came over to wish Teara a Happy Birthday." Vinnie said trying to act innocent.

Something was up, Teara thought. Vinnie wouldn't come over just to say something nice.

"Thanks." Teara said, treading carefully.

"Did you get something from your dear old Daddy?" Wanda asked, as innocently as she could manage.

Both Teara and Sophelia were now sure that something was wrong. Everyone knew that Teara didn't live with her family. And as far as Teara knew, there were only three people that knew that Philon had come to the school, other than herself. And she also knew that none of those three would blab.

"Or was he too busy ruining another hundred lives?" Trix snarled.

"How dare you!" Sophelia said, her short temper flaring into an inferno.

Teara now realized what everyone had been whispering about in the corridors. Her worst fears had happened.

"Ahh, watch out! Her father's anger streak might come out." Vinnie sniped. The twins laughed and they went back to their seats.

Teara was gob smacked. All this time she was trying to hide the truth from everyone, but now her whole year knew. And pretty soon the whole school would know. How had Vinnie and the clones found out?

"Teara. It'll be alright. Don't let this spoil..." Sophelia started.

"All right class. Settle down." Alfred said. He had walked in without Teara and Sophelia noticing.

Considering that the whole class knew about Teara's family tree, the lesson went pretty smoothly.

Alfred taught the class a new technique. It was called the Astro-projection Ability. When you used it, you could create up to three solid clones of yourself. This technique could be used to escape from an enemy. The downside was, it only lasted for a few seconds.

"That will come in handy when Teara's dear old daddy comes to visit." Vinnie had whispered across the class. Instantly making Teara drop back down into her dark cloud of depression. A cloud that seemed to stick to her more and more lately.

After a small dinner, Teara and Sophelia went to the forest. However they did not go to the Pond of *Tsaoil* as Sophelia was adamant that Teara would not go near there till the time of her party. They went to another small clearing instead and, careful to not get spotted by any over passing Griffins, they sat in the middle of it.

When they were about to leave a flame mail arrived for Teara. It was from her father.

"What do you know? He remembered today was my birthday." Teara said being sarcastic.

To My Dearest Daughter, Teara.

Happy Birthday. Inside this letter, your present had been wrapped.

I realize that when I last saw you, you must have been very surprised, and so you made a rash decision not to come and live with me. I am giving you another chance. If you wish to live with me please return this letter and I will come to pick you up.

Happy Birthday.
Your father.

Teara looked on the ground to where the present had fallen. She picked it up. It was a perfect dagger. In its hilt lay an encrusted red ruby. Teara grabbed the sting ray hilt and felt the weight of the blade. The blade was perfectly balanced. When Alfred had Teara trained in the martial arts, Teara had learned to fight with weapons, she had always preferred the smaller weapons, which could be easily concealed. She like how even though they were small and appeared pretty they were as deadly as the bigger ones.

After showing the dagger and note to Sophelia, Teara sheathed the dagger in its brown leather sheath and stuck it in her belt. She then pocketed the note, and in silence, the two girls started off to the pond of *Tsaoil*.

When they arrived there they saw the Nymph's huts were decorated with various pretty flowers. There was a bonfire in the middle and tables of food were scattered around. At one end of the semi-circle was a stage with a microphone and various instruments. There were a group of people scattered around, the whole nymph tribe was here.

When everyone saw Teara they yelled, "HAPPY

BIRTHDAY!!!" Teara found herself surrounded. After a while some of the Nymphs went to dance around the bonfire, their bodies making dance moves that no human could ever hope to make.

After Teara had been greeted by every person there, including Alfred who has braved his fear of the forest to be with her today, Teara opened her presents. Sophelia had given her a blue necklace with a matching blue bracelet she had made herself, which sparkled in the light of the bonfire, she instantly loved it and showed her gratitude by giving Sophelia along hug.

Teara also got some new school books from Alfred, a box of flame mail matches from Rosemi and a silk handkerchief which was shyly handed to her by Thorn, and just as shyly received.

Teara and Sophelia happily threw Philon's letter on the fire, but something made Teara decide to keep the dagger, possibly the overwhelming feeling that danger was coming. They then ate some of the various food from the buffet table, gorging themselves on the mouth-watering delicacies that lay before them. Surprisingly, it wasn't long before Teara was enjoying herself, and it was then that all the depressing feelings that had hung around her for the past couple of weeks evaporated. Chased away by the love and happiness she, her friends and her family had created together.

The sky was starting to darken. Everyone was sitting in a circle around the bonfire singing songs from years ago. There was one about some girl travelling over mountains and the sea, another about being married and a bike, and one that seemed to be mainly made of the words, *let it be*. This was the first time Teara actually got to see who was there.

Alfred was there, considering he didn't like the forest, he seemed to be enjoying himself. Rosemi was there, leading the singing with her beautiful voice.

Thorn was there as well, also singing, and blushing at the same time when he noticed Teara's eyes upon him. Ivy was there, and he nodded his head, before carrying on singing in his low tenor. The whole tribe was there. Sophelia was sitting beside Teara, her voice dry from singing too much. Once the song ended, Sophelia spoke.

"Teara, sing us a song."

"Uh. Nah." Teara said, aware of Thorns eyes on her.

"Go on. Sing us that lullaby you were telling me about." Sophelia said.

"Come on Teara. We've each chosen a song, it's your turn now." Rosemi smiled.

"Oh OK." Teara replied. She opened her mouth and started to sing, her voice scratchy on the high notes, and she consciously kept trying to keep her voice on the notes, singing was not her best talent.

"When the sun refuses to shine,
When the moon you cannot find,
When the tears start falling from our eyes,
remember I am here.

Even though the sky may fall,
and the stars may too,
but I will be here to take care of you.

We may live in a time of darkness,
but you are the light that shines,
somewhere through all this despair,
it is hope and love that we can find.

Even if the trees don't grow,
if we live in a world without snow,
I just want you to know,
I'm here for you.

The bangs of guns,
the blasts and shocks of bombs,
the devil and his henchmen,
cannot touch you while I am here.

So even if the fire refuses to burn,
and the rivers refuse to flow,
even if the wind refuses to blow,
you will never be alone,
for I will always be with you,
in your mind, heart and spirit,
I will always be with you."

As Teara ended the song everyone clapped. It was now midnight and a comet could be seen lighting up the sky. It was at this exact moment that a green light surrounded Teara and she could feel herself changing. Her body rippled in pain, every nerve felt as though it was burning. Teara couldn't help but let loose a scream of pain, but once the excruciating burning had receded it was replaced with that pleasant sensation that often followed after pins and needles. Once the green light had disappeared, everyone around Teara seemed to be much taller, and they all seemed to glow. She tried to talk, but no sound would come out. It was then that she looked at herself. She had turned into a Naturne, she lifted what felt like her right arm and her right wing responded, opening in all its beauty. Teara could only look at it in awe and wonder.

There was a gasp of awe and admiration from the tribe, Alfred and Sophelia. Then they all clapped again. Once again the pain engulfed her and Teara returned to her human form.

She was curled up in the foetal position with sweat pouring off her forehead. She looked over at Ivy and he smiled at her and nodded his head. Teara then heard his voice in her head, she was sure no one else could hear him as his lips weren't moving.

"Well done Teara. You have been gifted with the powers of a Naturne. I will help you learn how to control them. I have much to teach and show you." Teara nodded her head towards him and thought clearly;

"Will it always be that painful?" She asked.

"Nothing in life is free, in order to change form, a great deal of pain must be felt, you will never grow used to the pain, but the rewards are great!"

Teara nodded her head again in understanding, she couldn't wait to learn more.

<Chapter 17>

A Minor Victory

"Alright class, settle down." Alfred clapped his hands as the class started to calm. It was the last day of school before the Easter holidays, and the class were excited for their last Power Studies lesson of the term.

The class were in a long room with a long, thin red carpet running down one side of it, whilst the rest of the floor was made up of polished mahogany planks. Half of Teara's year stood beside the carpet, which Alfred stood upon. There was no furniture in the room, only a few paintings on the walls added to the sparse decoration.

This was going to be a special Power Studies lesson. At the end of each term, two students were chosen to use the powers they had learnt against one another in a safe setting. Alfred saw it as a bit of fun for his students as well as an opportunity for him to see how they were advancing in his class, and as no one except him knew who would be chosen, everyone would have to practice in order to be at the top of the game.

The class was now quiet, waiting with bated breath, with barely held anticipation to see who would be chosen.

"And it looks like the pair who will be showing us what we have learnt this term is...Sophelia Jenkings and Vinnie Stocksworthy." Alfred said. Teara looked at her friend to see Sophelia's face light up.

"Wish me luck." She whispered, grinning. Sophelia walked over to the red carpet, where Vinnie was already standing, glaring in her direction.

Teara knew her friend had been waiting for an opportunity like this for a long time. Since they had started attending the academy, Vinnie had been causing them nothing but trouble, always making snide remarks and hurting them whenever an opportunity presented itself. For Sophelia, this bullying had gotten worse when Vinnie learnt of her crush on Calumeno. Vinnie's anger only grew when Calumeno seemed to be showing interest in Sophelia. Teara knew Sophelia would never hurt Vinnie physically, but humiliating her in class would only hurt her ego.

"The loser gives up all claims on Calumeno." Vinnie whispered, shaking Sophelia's hand.

"You're on." Sophelia replied. The two girls then walked back the ten steps required so they could take their positions.

"On the count of three, you may begin your demonstration." Alfred said, "One...two...three!" Alfred stepped off the carpet to leave more room for the two girls. Any powers the two used would be restrained to the area of the carpet. By doing this, Alfred could also see their control over the powers the two demonstrated. The room lay in silence. Both of the girls just stood staring at each other, it wasn't until Sophelia raised an eyebrow that Vinnie made the first move. She put her hand to the sky, saying,

"*Ceo nacht!*" A white fog flooded the room. Teara could barely see the stage. This was one of the few powers that couldn't be restricted to the carpet, meaning the whole class had to respond in order to continue viewing the demonstration.

"*Glan radharc.*" Sophelia's voice flooded the room. Teara whispered the same. Immediately she could see through the fog to the carpet, the fog now only a cloudy circle around her vision.

"*Néarog rois.*" Vinnie screamed, a purple light shooting from her hand, at Sophelia. Sophelia dodged the light, immediately countering,

"*Téigh thart ar slabrai.*" Teara smiled as a chain made out of glass started to circle Vinnie. This had been the hardest power they had learnt. If the words were pronounced correctly, the wielder could encircle whomever they wanted in a chain made of glass, prohibiting the captures movements.

"*Ion chroi cosain.*" Vinnie shrieked on panic. The pink light pushed the chain away before disintegrating, Vinnie couldn't hold on to the memory needed to sustain the shield.

"*Sniomh airgead néal.*" Sophelia said, a burst of air shot out of Sophelia's hand, swirling the fog Vinnie created into a spinning cloud with Vinnie in the middle of it. Sweat had started to bead on Sophelia's forehead at the effort of having to keep the wind solely around Vinnie. Occasionally the wind ruffled one of the students who stood near the carpet, in doing so breaking the rule of keeping powers limited to the area of the red carpet.

"*Caoch éadroma!*" Vinnie screeched. A bright white light blinded Sophelia, leaving her temporarily sightless as she knelt on the carpet rubbing her eyes. Just as Vinnie was about to speak, Alfred interrupted.

"OK, well done. Now what did we learn from that?" Alfred asked, getting up onto the stage. He helped Sophelia to her feet before placing his hands on the two girl's shoulders.

"No one? Well we learned to never let our guard down. To always keep an eye on your opponent and never, never give up. Sophelia kept on the offensive, never giving up, but this cost her, she quickly lost her energy. Whilst Vinnie remained on the defensive, keeping an eye on her opponent, however, ou must all practice your pronunciation. Screaming the words will often lead to mispronunciation and then to the wrong or no magic being summoned. Well done girls. Class dismissed."

As the students started to make their way out of the door. Teara made her way through the crowd to Sophelia.

"Hey Teara." Sophelia said, obviously her sight was returning, though she did sound out of breath.

"What did you think of the fight then?" She asked.

"Um. Well it's a demonstration not a fight but I thought it was absolutely amazing." Teara replied, proud to be Sophelia's friend.

"Thanks, let's get going. I'm feeling a bit better now."

The two girls exited the room, into the entrance hall, they walked out of the oak doors and across to the field, as they wanted to study and both of them found that a lot easier to do outdoors. Just as they were settling down in the middle of the field, a shadow was cast over them. Sophelia and Teara looked up expecting a cloud to have passed in front of the sun.

Standing there was Vinnie, Wanda and Trix. Teara sighed, she wasn't in the mood for any more of Vinnie's sniping today. Especially since Teara had found out it was Vinnie and her crew who had been telling the whole school about her family heritage, putting a dark slant on Teara whilst doing so.

"Yes Vinnie." Teara said wearily.

"I want to continue my fight with Sophelia." Vinnie answered.

"Well maybe I don't want to. Besides it was a demonstration not a fight." Sophelia said.

"We don't care whether you want to or not, because either way you're going to." Wanda smirked.

It was clear that they weren't going to go away, which made Teara angry. These three girls has done their very best to make hers and Sophelia's lives a living misery. Even when Carlita had been here, they had practically tortures their lost friend. Carlita had been to gentle and soft to argue or fight back, merely agreeing with whatever insult Vinnie threw at her. This thought made Teara's anger spike. She could be studying, researching where to find her lost friend, how to get her back. But no. instead she was here having to listen to Vinnie start arguments like a spoilt brat, it was then that Teara made her decision.

"OK then. You want a fight. I'll fight for Sophelia." Teara said standing up.

"That's not fair. You're stronger than Vinnie. Plus you might have some secret Nymph powers that you could use against us!" Trix exclaimed.

"Yeah, or you'll fight dirty like your father. He's sure to have taught you some horrible fighting techniques." Wanda sneered.

"If you fight you have to fight all three of us" Vinnie said.

"Leave it Teara. There's no way you can beat all three of them. Plus what would Alfred say if he heard you of all people had been fighting?" Sophelia asked, starting to worry about Teara.

"I know. But they are clearly not going to leave us alone until we fight. Even if I don't win, I won't go down easy and where possible, I'll take them down with me." Teara replied, realizing how much like her father she sounded, but no longer caring. People will believe what they want to believe, and there was nothing she could do about it. Vinnie and the twins smirked. Sophelia could just here one of them whisper "There's no way she can beat us."

"Let's get to it then." Vinnie said. Trix, Wanda and Vinnie were now circling Teara. Teara quickly grew bored with the circling and tried to goad them into action.

"Were you three vultures in another life?" She

asked, raising her eyebrow in question.

Immediately the three girls stopped circling, they looked at each other and shouted in unison, "*Pairilis canoin!*" Three identical yellow beams of light were shot at Teara, forming a big sphere of yellow light around her. The three girls held the beams steady for a couple seconds, which felt like hours to Sophelia. When the trio finally took away the beams and the light had disappeared the now gathering crowd gasped. Where merely moments ago Teara had stood, was nothing.

"Where did she go?" Vinnie shouted, looking around at the crowd. Sophelia's concerned face also searching the crowd for her friend.

"Looking for me?" Teara said tapping Vinnie on the shoulder. Vinnie turned around and looked at Teara in amazement.

"But...How...You..." Wanda stammered. Teara laughed, rolling her eyes.

"You're wondering how I got here. Well, let me educate you, while you three were circling me, I simply shivered out moments before your hidden magic hit me." Teara said nonchalantly.

"So that thing we blasted was a dud." Trinnie said.

"I guess you could say that. Though it would be more accurate to say that you didn't blast anything." Teara smiled.

"Enough chat! "*Eitilte scean ionsai!*" Vinnie shouted and the twins copied. Hundreds of knives now flew at Teara. Teara avoided them by performing a couple of back flips and a cartwheel, then pointed her hand at them and said, "*Peiteal Claochlaigh!*" The knives changed into beautiful purple rose petals that gently drifted to the ground, in front of the students who has come to watch. Teara's rage again peaked at the carelessness of Vinnie. Didn't she realize that those knives may have not just hurt her, but any number of onlookers as well?

"Damn." Vinnie said.

"My move," Teara said, disappearing in a spiral of leaves.

"Careful girls. She could attack any one of us." Vinnie warned.

The crowd was now silent, listening for any sound that would tell them what was going to happen next. The air was thick with tension.

"Wait! Where's Wanda?! Trix's voice reached Sophelia from the crowd. Both Vinnie and Trix started looking around, trying to find Trix's twin.

Just then Teara's voice echoed across the grounds. Sophelia tried to pin point it, but she couldn't. It seemed to be coming from everywhere.

"Wanda is with me. If you want her back, you'll have to end the fight."

"Trying to be like your father now Teara!?" Vinnie shouted. "Who are you planning to kidnap next?"

"No one." Teara's cold voice could barely be heard, it was barely above a whisper. Sophelia could hear just how angry her friend was in that one word. She had never heard Teara sound so cold.

"*Sci stoirm nacht.*" Teara shouted. Vinnie and Trix closed their eyes and covered their faces with their arms in preparation against the onslaught of ice. After a momentary pause they opened their eyes, wondering at the lack of ice.

"Ha! It didn't work." Trix shouted back at Teara, who had now reappeared in front of them.

"Didn't it." Teara raised her eyebrows, "Turn around." The two girls, very slowly, turned around. A roar erupted from the panther, which was made of ice, before it melted. Fear was in Vinnie's eyes. It took a lot of focus and energy to mould an ice storm into a creature. Trix screamed.

"What...what is it?" Vinnie looked to where Trix was looking. Her face turned white.

In front of them was a giant serpent made of ice, and wrapped within its coils was Wanda. Trix turned to Teara.

"What have you done with her? Give her back!" Tears were in Trix's eyes.

"She is asleep. She'll wake up as soon as this pointless fight is over. You let your guard down. Now you find yourself in an impossible situation. You could carry on fighting and risk Wanda getting hurt. Or you could give up and let your twin walk away unscathed."

Both Vinnie and Trix gasped.

"You wouldn't." Vinnie exclaimed.

"Wouldn't what? Let Wanda stay there while we fight? True, I wouldn't leave her there. I'd just trap her in a chain so she wouldn't get hurt. But still accidents happen." Teara snapped her fingers and the serpent melted leaving Wanda lying in the wet grass. Teara sighed "I would've thought that you'd have wanted to save Wanda. However...I wouldn't expect you to save your friends. You don't have the common decency or compassion to do something so selfless." Teara looked at Vinnie coldly. Vinnie shuddered under the gaze, then smiled.

"Maybe...Maybe not. It all depends on what's to be gained if I win the fight. Like in this case, losing isn't an option. *'Dóiteáin dragan anáil'* Fire erupted out of Vinnie's mouth, aiming straight for Teara. Teara only just dodged it, part of her uniform being singed in the process.

"Trix help me out." Vinnie ordered. Trix shook her head and ran over to her twin. Teara watched as Trix picked up Wanda's unconscious body in her arms. Trix looked at Teara, her eyes pleading for this to end. Teara nodded in understanding. There was no hope asking her friend to end this, Vinnie was too selfish for that. So Trix had taken the only option open to her, asking the person who she had bullied to help.

"*Caoch éadroma*" The white light stopped Vinnie from seeing Teara, and that gave Teara just the advantage she wanted. Teara shivered over to Vinnie.

"*Sniomh airgead néal*" The burst of air erupted out of Teara's hands until, once again, Vinnie was trapped.

"What is this?" Vinnie screeched.

Teara took away the tornado of air and, before Vinnie could do more than look at her, Teara had one of Vinnie's arms behind her back and her throat under her father's dagger, which she had unsheathed from her leg holster moments before.

"Tell them you give." Teara whispered.

"I give." Vinnie whispered back.

"So they can hear you."

"I give!" Vinnie shouted. The crowd burst into cheers. Teara released Vinnie, who went over to the twins. Wanda awakening in Trix's arms.

That was when Teara heard it. The same mysterious whisper. The crowd's cheers faded into the background as Teara listened.

"Teara...Teara...come and find me."

"Where?" Teara whispered.

"I'm in the forest." The whisper answered. Teara started to walk over to the forest. She pushed past the crowd, hoping she would not meet anyone she would have to talk to. Unfortunately, the odds were against here.

"Teara, well done." Sophelia said, going to give Teara a hug when her friends raised hand stopped her.

"I'll see you later." Teara said, not stopping.

"But..." Sophelia started.

"Later." Teara interrupted. Sophelia stopped dead as

Teara continued walking. When Teara reached the forest, and was hidden from the crowd, she spoke.

"Where about in the forest?" She asked the surrounding air.

"In the Griffin clearing. By the river." The whisper answered. Teara shivered to the clearing and was walking down the river when she heard a voice.

"Teara, what are you doing here?" Teara turned, her heart falling as she saw it was Rosemi.

"Oh nothing." Teara said, praying Rosemi didn't see her eyes change colour. But Rosemi was too busy looking at Teara's leg. Teara looked down. It was badly burned. Must of happened with the Dragon Fire, she thought.

"Come on. I'm taking you back to the Pond of *Tsaoil* to get that leg sorted. I'm surprised you can walk." Rosemi stated. Teara was about to protest when she thought better of it.

"OK." She said instead. Rosemi held Teara's hand and shivered them both back to the Pond of *Tsaoil*, intending to find out just exactly how her charge has received such a burn.

<Chapter 18>

Feather

It wasn't long until the last day of the holidays dawned. Teara's leg had been fully healed by Rosemi, who had given her a lecture about fighting, a lecture which had been repeated by Alfred the moment he found out. Though she had later found out that he had been secretly watching the fight from his office window, and was proud of the powers, skills and control Teara had shown.

Teara hadn't seen Sophelia since the fight, she wasn't avoiding her friend but her mind had been elsewhere. Thoughts of the whisper that only she could hear, of trying to find Carlita, worrying over what her family was doing next and how it was going to impact her and those she loved. However, she had received a flame mail from Sophelia saying thanks for sticking up for her, and that her family were taking her to Wales for the holiday, so it wasn't entirely down to Teara that the two hadn't seen one another.

So Teara had spent the holiday on her own. Well, as alone as you could be with the; Nymphs, Permanent students, Alfred and the creatures of the forest.

However it wasn't these things that kept Teara occupied through the holiday. Researching all of her worries was what took up her time. She spent hours at a time researching what could have happened to Carlita, something that wasn't bringing any results. Everything she read just raised more questions instead of answers. Whenever a newspaper was abandoned she was reading it to find out the latest crimes that her father had committed, and of course she was desperately trying to find the source of the whisper. Something she could swear was driving her to insanity for, every time Teara came close to finding out what it was, she was interrupted.

Out of desperation more than anything, Teara decided to go meet some of her Centaur friends to see if they could tell her what the whisper was, after all, Centaur's were one of the most mysterious creatures so they were bound to know something.

So that is how it came to be that Teara was walking around the forest, searching for the Centaurs, on the last day of the holidays. It wasn't till around noon that Teara finally got lucky. Through the dense trees she could see three Centaurs. One with a pale white body and white hair that flowed out behind him, one had a chestnut body and very short brown hair whilst the third was black all over with shoulder length locks. They were all riding away from her.

"Mecur...Jasper...Sombrien!" Teara called. The three Centaurs stopped and looked over at Teara, trotting over once they had identified her. Centaurs liked to name their children after the stars and planets they spent so long looking at or the stones they spent all day collecting. It had taken Teara ages to learn how to pronounce all the different names.

"Well look who it is." The black centaur said to the other two.

"If it isn't little Teara." The brown one teased.

"Not so little anymore Mecur." Teara replied.

"Mm. True. Last time we saw you, you were no bigger than a toddler." The third centaur said smiling at her.

"So...what's up?" Mecur asked.

"Nothing." Teara said simply. Now that she'd found them, she was having second thoughts about telling the centaurs about the whisper. She was already thought of as something different, surely saying she heard voices would set her further apart?

"Well the look on your face says different." The black centaur, Sombrien, contradicted.

"Come on, you can tell us," Jasper reassured her, gently nudging her shoulder with his fist.

"OK. Well I've been hearing this whisper..." Teara started hesitantly but before she could explain any more, the three centaurs interrupted her.

"Oh hearing voices is bad."
"Very bad."
"You could be crazy. Oh sorry, my mistake, you already are." Mecur laughed, ever the comedian of the group.

"Ha ha, Mecur." Teara said sarcastically.

"Well carry on." Sombrien encouraged her. Teara told them all about the whisper and all the times she had heard it. She told them how she had tried to find the source of the whisper, but was always interrupted. How it seemed that only she could hear it, and how she was pretty certain the whisper was female.

"Mmm. I think we better bring you to Lutarsin." Jasper announced, after Teara had finished.

"L...Lutarsin!" Teara had only seen Lutarsin once, when she was younger, and that was only so he could give his approval of a human living in the forest, as Lutarsin was the head of the centaur herd that resided in the forest. Without his approval there could have been a lot of strife between the herd and the academy. If she was honest, Lutarsin scared her.

"You want to find out about this whisper, don't you?" Mecur asked.

"Yes." Teara replied. If there was one thing she wanted at this precise moment in time, it was to know about the whisper. And if that meant going to Lutarsin, then she would swallow her fear and go.

"OK then, hop on." Sombrien instructed her,

lowering his arm to help. Teara grabbed his arm and, with his help, hopped up onto his back, sitting side saddle.

"No need to ask you to hold on, I suppose, not with your great sense of balance." Sombrien murmured sarcastically.

"Did you say something Sombrien?" Teara asked innocently.

"No. Come on guys."

The three centaurs started to gallop off into the forest. Teara tried to sit and enjoy the ride but her mind kept wandering, worrying over the same three issues that continued to circle in her head; Carlita, whisper, family, Carlita, whisper, family. Over and over again.

Lutarsin must have changed since their last acquaintance. Sure centaurs lived to around two hundred years of age, but they can't stay the same for that whole time. That was impossible, wasn't it? They had to age. Even Rosemi aged slightly and she was practically immortal.

"Business?"

"We are here to see Lutarsin." Sombrien stated. Teara was taken away from her thoughts, by the guard's gruff voice. Sombrien was talking to a grey centaur, who had a spear in his hand. Teara's hand flinched towards her dagger at the sight of the sharp end of the spear, but she stopped herself just in time. Luckily the guard hadn't noticed, his focus entirely upon the three centaurs who accompanied her.

"Why?" The guard asked.

"None of your business. This girl has private affairs of which she can only talk to Lutarsin about." Sombrien sounded very official all of a sudden.

The grey centaur whispered to another centaur behind him which disappeared through the leafy ark, made by tree branches woven together, it created an opening in the otherwise impenetrable wall of old oak trees.

A couple of minutes passed. All was silent and a crowd of centaurs had begun to gather in curiosity at why this stranger wanted to talk to their leader. The crowd was all staring at Teara. It was not often that the herd saw humans, let alone in their forest, it wasn't long till they began to break into whispers, discussing this development. The centaur that had left through the ark returned, whispered into the guard's ear and then left again.

"Thank you for waiting. Lutarsin will see you now." The guard said to Teara, Sombrien, Mecur and Jasper.

The small group went through the arch, Teara whispering a small thank you to the guard as they passed. The guard just stuck up his nose, clearly not liking the fact that a human was being allowed to speak to Lutarsin.

The darkness of a leafy tunnel enveloped the small group, when they had reached the end, they walked through another arch of woven leaves and tree branches, entering a well-lit clearing, and it took Teara's eyes a few moments to adjust to the sudden brightness.

Teara blinked. In the middle of the clearing was a small mound. Upon the mound stood a beautiful mustard coloured centaur. He was Lutarsin. The centaur put up a hand and beckoned the group to him. The three centaurs walked timidly towards the mound where their leader stood. Once there, thanking Sombrien, Teara slid off her back, gracefully kneeling into a curtsy while the other centaurs bowed their heads, left arms crossed to their right shoulders in a sign of respect.

"Sombrien...Mecur...Jasper... How dare you bring a human into my midst! What do you mean by it?" The centaur commanded. His voice low and treacherous, sounding like ice scraping against stone.

'I was wrong' Teara thought. Lutarsin hadn't changed one bit. He was as proud and as stubborn as ever. Listening to no one but himself, and only trusting his own judgement, even before he had heard the circumstances.

"This human is Teara Dream. And she wants to ask your advice on something." Mercur announced.

Teara looked at Lutarsin's face, searching for any sign of emotion.

"Well...That changes everything!" Lutarsin's strict face broke into a smile. Teara was shocked. But she hid her emotions by timidly returning his smile.

"Teara tell me what you want my advice for." Lutarsin said. Teara once again repeated the story of the whisper, and what she had concluded on her own. After she had finished, Lutarsin remained quiet for a moment. Then his loud voice broke the silence.

"Very interesting. Well first of all...I want you three to leave." He said pointing at Sombrien, Mecur and Jasper.

"But...But why?" Jasper protested.

"My advice is for Teara's ears only. Please leave us." Lutarsin replied.

Mecur bowed. "As you wish." He said leading his two friends away and, walking together, they exited the clearing through the same arch they had entered.

Lutarsin turned toward Teara. She bowed her head before looking up to meet his ginger eyes, which seemed full of wonder, knowledge and untold mysteries.

"My advice for you, Teara, is to find an abandoned clearing, preferably in this forest." Lutarsin's face had turned from friendly and carefree to strictly serious. "Stay there. Alone. Wait for the whisper to call you again. When it does wait where you are. Do not follow it. If my suspicions are correct, the thing casting the voice will come to you, but only if you are alone." Lutarsin finished.

Teara nodded her head. She thanked the leader of the centaurs before disappeared in a spiral of leaves. Mecur, Sombrien and Jasper trotted back into the clearing.

"Is it what we thought?" Jasper asked, receiving no answer from Lutarsin, only a nod of his head.

***

Teara reappeared in a completely deserted clearing of the forest. She had only ever visited this clearing once before, however on that occasion she had been accompanied by around twenty adult Nymphs and other than that once they had never visited again.

This time Teara was all by herself, surrounded by an eerie circling mist that was very intimidating. After all, this particular part of the forest was completely uninhabited because of the mist. The mist had strange magical properties which repelled any living creature away from it. So creatures rarely visited and, when they did, they never stayed for too long.

Teara was hoping to be one of those who didn't stay longer than they needed to. She had only chosen this spot because it was deserted, that way the caster of the voice might reveal themselves sooner rather than later.

Teara sat on a rock and made herself comfortable, if she had to wait long she might as well have somewhere where her legs wouldn't cramp.

Time passed...Five minutes....ten....half an hour...an hour...Teara started to hum to herself, she wasn't lonely, just bored.

Soon two hours had passed. Just as Teara thought

that this was starting to seem pointless, a cold wind buffeted her, the whisper just heard within its icy embrace. As abruptly as it came, this wind dissipated.

Teara looked up. Just beyond the mist she could make out a shadow. Teara steadied her breathing. The power emanating from this person or creature was palpable.

"Teara...I have been looking for you...And finally we meet." The creature spoke in a mystic voice, unlike anything Teara had ever heard.

Teara tried to speak but no sound came out. It was like she had been frozen. An ankle and foot appeared out of the mist. No that wasn't right. Not out of it but more like the mist joined together to create the ankle and foot. Then slowly the mist conjoined to create the rest of the creature.

It was a woman. Or what looked like a woman at least. It had very light brown hair reaching to halfway down it's back, the hair was floating in the surrounding air. Sparkling green eyes stared at Teara. A smile was on the creature's pale face. The sky blue body length dress that wrapped around her petite stature flapping in the breeze.

"It is nice to finally meet you, Teara." The creature said again, her voice clearer now, sounded like a pure gentle breeze, the type you could hear among the tree branches. It was remembering that breeze that she had grown up with that helped Teara to finally find her voice.

"What are you?" Teara had come to a decision. There was no way this creature was human. For one thing it didn't seem to walk but lightly float a centimetre off the ground. As if the mist that had created her also supported her weight. The creature gave a light laugh.

"I am a daughter of the wind. One of five from a

prophecy made long ago. My name is Feather." It just so happened that Teara had heard of the prophecy in question. It was one that was told as a story around campfires. However that prophecy had a good many years till it was due to be fulfilled, it had already been around for centuries. If what this creature said was true then one question remained.

"Why have you shown yourself to me then?" Teara asked. Her hand behind her back in preparation in case she needed to reach for her dagger.

"Because a danger is coming. And you are one of those needed to stop it." Feather replied.

Without consciously knowing it Teara let her arm drop, returning limply to her side. Somehow, and Teara didn't know how herself, she knew this 'being' was telling the truth.

"M-Me" Teara stammered.

"Yes you." Feather said, a smile flashing across her porcelain features. Teara couldn't take it in. So many questions were whirring inside her.

"But why me?"

"I cannot answer that question yet." Feather answered.

"But what if I can't do it?"

"But..." Feather started but Teara interrupted.

"How can you tell it's me you need?"

"I can tell because..."

"What is this danger that is coming?"

"The danger..."

"Who is it that is in danger?"

"Teara you..."

"Is it me?"

"Teara..."

"Or someone I know?"

"You know Teara language has a brother." Feather shouted over Teara's questions. In spite of what was happened, Teara was intrigued.

"Really who?"

"He's called, silence!" Feather shouted and suddenly she seemed a lot more human. And that was when Teara realised something.

If Feather was a daughter of the wind then she was half human and so...she could be trusted.

"What is it you want me to do?" Teara asked in a quiet voice.

"Good girl." Feather said returning to her mystic tones. "I need to talk to you about an old friend of yours, one that goes by the name of Carlita..."

<Chapter 19>

Threatened

The sun shone from its place in the middle of the sky. Its rays warming up everything they touched. The light reached the pond of *Tsaoil*, glistening across the water. However there was no one around to see this pretty sight. For the nymphs had taken their little ones to visit the nymphs of Glasgow, a yearly gathering where two groups could mix, exchange gossip and teach their young how to socialize with their Scottish neighbours. The animals were at a gathering celebrating the birth of a new unicorn, an event that no one wanted to miss. The only sounds were those of the trees rustling in the gentle summer breeze. It was nearing the middle of summer and the last week of term was approaching.

A bell rang in the distance signalling that it was lunchtime. The students flooded out of the academy's gates, down the steps to bask in the warm sunshine. Amongst the flood of children was Sophelia and Teara. Sophelia's face was alight with laughter at a joke the two had just shared.

"Shall we go somewhere quiet?" Sophelia asked after she had recovered from her laughing fit.

"Why not?" Teara replied. It had been two weeks since she had met the daughter of the wind, Feather. Teara had yet to confide in Sophelia about what had happened, and didn't plan to until she felt the time was right. Summer was Sophelia's favourite season, and Teara couldn't bring herself to shatter her friend's joy just yet.

"Question is..." Teara started to say.

"Where shall we go?" Sophelia finished. She pulled a face mimicking a person thinking extremely hard.

"Well it's not like there is a 12 acre plot for students to wander around in the school, though most of that is going to be filled with students. There is definitely not a school behind us with practically hundreds of empty classrooms, but who would want to be indoors when there is this glorious sunshine? And I know for a fact there isn't a giant forest, right over there. Where very few students tend to go!" Sophelia said pointing in the direction of the forest. Teara laughed. She got Sophelia's point.

"Race you then!" She said as she ran off towards the forest.

"Hey no fair, you know you're better than me at sports." Sophelia yelled before running after her. The two girls barged past the students who walked across their path, weaving in between those who yelled at them. As Sophelia predicted, Teara reached the forest first. Teara lent against a tree, barely out of breath, waiting for Sophelia to catch up.

"Y...you d...did that o...on purpose!" Sophelia stammered trying to catch her breath. "You know today is the one day of the school week that I don't do sports." Sophelia said finding her voice. Teara pulled a really innocent face.

"Oh I didn't realise." She said in a high squeaky voice. "On the other hand exercise is good for you." Sophelia smiled and lightly hit Teara across the head, earning a laugh from her friend.

"Bit feisty today are we?" Teara teased jumping into a nearby tree.

"Awww no fair, you know I can't do that." Sophelia whined. Teara swung from tree to tree, looking almost like a monkey, until she was slowly heading down the path. Sophelia sighed at her friend's choice of travel and, taking the more original route of walking, followed Teara down the path.

Back at the pond of *Tsaoil* the silence was shattered by the two girl's laughter. Sophelia walked into the clearing and Teara jumped from a tree to land just behind her. Together they walked to the pond, took off their shoes and paddled their feet into the water. The cool water easing their aching feet and giving them a pleasant chill in the otherwise hot summer sun. They sat there a while chatting before getting out some sandwiches and eating them.

For a while they talked about trivial matters, what homework they had done, how Sophelia couldn't believe that Calumeno had asked her over his for dinner later that week. They both marvelled at the fact that since the fight between Vinnie and Teara, the trio had been leaving them alone. Sure there was the whispers behind hands, occasional barging in the halls and rumour mongering behind their back, but there has been no more face to face confrontations. Teara speculated that this may have been down to Alfred having a word with the trio. She had never told him about the bullying that has occurred but since the fight he has been questioning both her and Sophelia onto why it had occurred. It was only a matter of time till he pieced the truth together.

"Can you hear that?" Sophelia asked. With a puzzled look on her face.

"Hear what" Teara replied puzzled.

"That buzzing sound." Sophelia said. Teara listened carefully. If she ignored the trickle of the waterfall and all the other usual sounds that inhabited the forest she could indeed hear a faint, out of place, buzzing sound. It was like a group of bees.

"Yeah, what do you think it could be?" She asked.

"I don't know, go up and find out." Sophelia answered, receiving a confused look from her friend.

"And what do you mean by that?" Teara questioned.

"Well, as you clearly proved the whole way here, you are a marvellous tree climber, so go over to that large oak on the other side of the clearing, clamber up and see what's going on!" Sophelia said in exasperation.

"Oh ok," Teara replied smiling, she ran over to the tree and jumped at the nearest branch, pulling herself up. She steadily, easily and gracefully identified handholds and started her climb up the tree. Even though she enjoyed climbing trees she really wished Ivy would hurry up and teach her how to change into her Naturne form. Flying up would be much quicker, not to mention would probably feel really special.

"Hurry up." Sophelia's voice reached Teara through the branches, she sounded worried, which unnerved Teara even more than it should have. She didn't make the mistake of looking down, she was too high up to do that.

Instead she just continued her ascent until she broke through the high branches. The bright sun assaulting her eyes, she had to blink a few times till they adjusted to the sudden change. She was facing the academy, a large building in the countryside, its red bricks reflecting the sun, giving the impression that he building was glowing. Little black dots moved around the grounds that surrounded the building, obviously students enjoying their lunch break.

Balancing herself on the branch, she slowly turned, surveying the familiar surroundings. It didn't take her long to identify the source of the buzzing. It was when her back was facing the academy that she spotted it. It wasn't bees or even wasps. There in the distant sky could be seen a row of black dots, standing out against the blue. Teara gasped.

Squinting her eyes she was able to identify these dots. They were Pegasus'. A large number of them, the beat of their wings creating the humming that Sophelia had heard. Each rider was riding double, and they were getting closer incredibly fast. Leading the group was a dappling grey Pegasus, carrying one rider with a black cloak. Teara would recognise that Pegasus anywhere. It was her fathers. The Dream Squad had chosen their next target.

Teara couldn't help but sway in mid-air. She had always thought that their academy would be safe. How could her own father attack the place where his daughter lived, when there would be a high risk of her getting hurt? Surely the basic fatherly instinct went against that. Apparently in Philon's case it didn't.

As fast as she could Teara descended the old oak, grazing skin on her elbows and knees in her rush to tell someone, anyone, what was happening.

When she reached the bottom, Sophelia took in her grazed skin, white face and shaking hands.

"Teara, what is it? You've gone so pale, why are you shaking?" Teara didn't reply, she just stood there swaying. Thoughts swirling through her head. Her father was here. With his followers. Speeding towards the academy in order to attack her home. Where hundreds of students were enjoying their lunch without the knowledge that they were in imminent danger. She had to tell someone, but who? Rosemi wasn't hear, and neither was Lutarsin and Alfred was...That was it. She would tell Alfred. He would be in his office. He had to be in his office, it was her only hope.

"Teara..." Sophelia looked worried. Her face a mixture of concern and confusion.

"Alfred, we need to get to Alfred this instant!" Teara shouted.

"Buy why...?" Sophelia started to ask, but she was too late. Teara had already grabbed her hand and the familiar sensation of leaves spiralling around them as

Teara shivered them both to inside Alfred's office

***

Alfred had been spending his lunch hour marking papers, he had to teach next period and would rather do them during lunch and then have a relatively free evening. So when Teara shivered herself into his office, without even knocking, near the end of the lunch hour he was very annoyed. Especially when he took in the bewildered expression on Sophelia's face, obviously he wasn't the only one who didn't like this turn of events.

"What is the meaning of this Teara? You know you should knock first. This is completely...Teara are you alright?" Alfred asked, taking in her pale face, wide eyes and deep breathing.

"Philon's here!" Teara exclaimed, her voice unnaturally high pitched.

"What! Calm down Teara, take a seat and tell me what is going on." Alfred gestured to a nearby seat, watching as Teara refused to take the seat, instead pacing across the floor as she described what she had seen. Sophelia fell into the chair in shock, whilst Alfred's look of concern grew into one of anger and worry.

Once Teara had finished telling Alfred about the oncoming attack, he stood up and bent to look out the window. He took in a deep, sharp breath as he saw the first few pegasus' appear over the distant trees of the forest. It was just as Alfred was standing up that another person burst uninvited into the office. He was the astrology teacher and he seemed completely calm on the outside but his panicked eyes and abrupt entrance betrayed him. Pualo Merdelie addressed his head teacher.

"Headmaster, he is here. Philon Dream has declared

that our academy is his next target."

"I have already become aware of this situation Merdelie, go to the assembly hall and wait there." Alfred instructed, and Pualo exited the office to go to the hall.

"Sophelia...Teara...go with him, wait in the hall and nowhere else. We need act quickly." With his instructions given, Alfred flipped a switch that lay under his desk. Instantly the sound of the school bell, except in a higher pitch and louder intensity, rang through the academy grounds. This bell was rarely used as it symbolized that everyone had to gather immediately in the hall.

At the sound of the bell, Teara and Sophelia left Alfred's office and ran as fast as they could to the hall. When they reached the bottom of the stairs they joined the crowds that were rushing into the hall, standing around as there wasn't anywhere to sit. On the stage stood Alfred, who had managed to reach the hall before the girls by using one of the many secret passageways that lay in the academy. Teara and Sophelia chose a spot near the entrance to stand, so that if needed they could exit quickly. As soon as the student body spotted Alfred they succumbed to immediate silence.

"I'm afraid I have had to call this emergency assembly to give you some very grave news." Alfred addressed his students and staff. Watching them all carefully to make sure no hysteria broke out. "Our beloved academy has been chosen as the Dream Squad's next target. Any minute now we will be under attack. Philon Dream, himself, is leading the charge which is almost on our doorstep. If you would all look at your hands, those who have been elected by their teachers will have the academy symbol shining on your palm. You have been chosen to help protect the school. However if you do not wish to, you will not be judged.

You may follow the rest of the student body to the underground bunker situated at the rear of the grounds. Students please follow your form teachers to the bunker now. Those with a symbol we will immediately convene in front of the academy. Dismissed." Without a backward glance, Alfred left the stage.

Students and teachers alike looked at their hands, some with dread some with excitement, those with a symbol, who wished to fight, made their way to the front of the academy as instructed. Everyone else was being gently herded through the entrance hall and out a back room, which had a secret tunnel leading to the bunker.

Both Teara and Sophelia looked down at their palms to find the academy symbol blazing brightly.

"Are you going to fight?" Teara asked her friend, hoping that she wouldn't. Lately she had been finding more and more information on her father, and she wasn't liking any of it.

"If you are, I am. I am not a coward and will always stay by your side. That's what friends are for. Besides I couldn't do anything to help Carlita, maybe there is something I could do to help you." Sophelia gave Teara a huge hug. It was the first sign she had shown that the kidnap of their old friend had deeply impacted her. She was always so cheerful and optimistic that Teara had often wondered if Sophelia was in denial about the whole thing. Turns out they both had been suffering silently. Teara vowed if she made it through this she would tell Sophelia everything, even what Feather had told her about their friend. An arm encircled the two girl's shoulders.

"Come on now you two, look on the bright side, if we go, at least we will be together. And I don't know about you but if I gotta go I want to go in style." Teara looked up to see Jessye, an upperclassman who had, on many occasions, helped the two with their homework. Jessye was smiling down at them, Teara and Sophelia couldn't help but smile back.

The three girls walked together to the front stairs, but as they did so, Teara couldn't help but notice Calumeno joining Vinnie and the twins as they left for the bunker, a bright symbol on his hand.

<Chapter 20>

Standing Strong

As Teara walked through the great oak doors, she looked up at the sky. The beautiful weather of the day had disappeared leaving a dark overcast sky, full of dark grey and black clouds in its place. A sharp wind had picked up, lashing the trees, making them bend under its power. The day had turned dark, almost as if the day had become night. The temperature had dropped, leaving a cold chill in the air that froze all in its path.

Teara and Sophelia had now reached the back of the gathering group of students, who had been deemed skilled enough to help defend the academy. The two girls carefully and politely made their way through the crowd to the front. The sight that met them had both girls staring in shock. The riders had arrived, each dismounting before their steed had landed, leaving the Pegasus to turn dangerously, flying off to the safe cover of the forest.

The two friends quickly made their way along the front line of students and staff until she found Alfred. He had placed himself in the center of the line, talking to the people on his sides. Beside Alfred was Jessye and another upperclassman called Mijak. Alfred was in deep conversation with the two. Mijak was almost an older version of Calumeno in being very attractive and popular with the female half of the student body. With intense blue eyes, a sharp jawline and spiky blond hair with blue tips, it was hard to think of him as ugly. When one took into account that he was top in the school for battle strategies it was no wonder that he and

Alfred were in deep conversation. They were probably discussing the best way to cunningly eliminate the threat with minimal danger and injury to the combatants.

"What's the plan?" Sophelia asked Alfred. Receiving a look and a deep sigh.

"All we can really do is fight to the best of our ability and hope to win." Alfred sighed.

"We don't have enough time to think up anything else, let alone make sure everyone knows it." Mijak said, with an apologetic smile. He looked over to see the enemy who was slowly growing in numbers.

"It's not your fault Mijak, no one is to blame." Jessye comforted her friend, placing her hand on his arm. It was then that Sophelia nudged Teara and Alfred. Both turned to where she was looking. There, directly opposite Alfred was Philon Dream, Teara's father. His dark grey eyes were scanning the crowd, his face a mixture of surprise and amusement. As his eyes fell upon Alfred and his daughter he smiled.

The two opposing crowds were now silent. The only sound was the whistling of the wind as it blew through the trees. Both groups were looking at the glare that passed between their two leaders. The glare showed the anger and hatred each man held for the other. For years they had fought against each other, and now that this brief period of calm had come to an end, it was like it had never occurred.

To Teara it looked as if the school grounds had been split into three. One crowd of students and staff, prepared to do all they could to protect their academy, and their fellow students who, if they failed, would face the wrath of this despicable group. The second was said despicable group, the

Dream Squad, with their leader showing them the way, all prepared to die for their beliefs in the hope of changing the world for their own gain. The third was situated behind the Dream Squad. It was the Nymphs who had returned from their outing to Glasgow. They were hidden just behind the trees, not entering the field. Rosemi and Thorn watching at the front of the group. Rosemi's hair blown to one side by the wind, she reminded Teara of a watchful goddess.

The Nymphs would not fight for it was not their battle. It was not their way to fight, when trouble arose they would merely disappear into their surroundings. They had only shown themselves now as a sign of support for Teara, for like her, they believed themselves to be a family.

The sound of a single person clapping slowly disturbed Teara from her thoughts. Looking over she saw that it was her father who was clapping in a slow condescending manner, a large grin plastered on his face.

"Well, well. Now isn't this interesting. Never before have I had a school come out to greet me. Usually they fight, oh yes they fight, but always when the end is near." Philon's voice was cold, devoid of all emotion.

"You are not welcome here Philon. Be gone. This academy will not sit idly by while you try to impose that ridiculous ideology of yours. I repeat. Go, you are not welcome here." Alfred's voice was calm and collected, his eyes, however, told a different story. His once calm and loving hazel brown eyes, now seethed with anger.

"Now, now, Mr. Pine. Is that any way to great an old friend?" Philon placed a hand over his heart playing wounded.

"If you were an old friend you would be welcomed most graciously, this greeting, on the other hand, is perfect for the old enemy you are." Teara could see Alfred's hand begin to shake as he spoke, she grasped his hand with hers, hoping she could give him strength. Unfortunately Philon noticed this small movement and his attention shifted from his enemy to his daughter.

"Ah, my darling daughter, Teara. How nice it is to see you again. But you seem to be misplace, come over here to your father and family. Come to the side of truth and justice. Come home daughter." Philon held out his hand. Teara couldn't believe he thought that she would actually do it. Of all the decisions she had made in her life, this was the easiest. She couldn't abandon her friends, her real family, for an ideology she didn't believe in.

"I am home. This is the side I belong." Teara spoke loud and clear, making sure her voice carried so that everyone would know her choice. Even know this man was her father, her flesh and blood, she didn't care. All Teara wanted was the people who had raised and loved her, the people who made up her real family.

"But you seem to be missing part of your family my dear, what about your friend Carlita?" Teara's face filled with shock at her father's words. She had to grasp Sophelia's arm to stop her from throwing herself at him in anger. Tears streamed down her friends face. Whether they were tears of anger or sadness, she did not know.

"Come to me know Teara before I have to force you. You wouldn't want to make your father angry." Philon's voice now mimicked ice, but Teara did not care.

"Then come over and force me. You're no father

of mine! I wouldn't come to you willingly if it was the last thing I did." Teara's statement brought out a chuckle from Mijak. She couldn't help but turn to him.

"Sorry, it's just I don't think you realise your daughter is a teenager. Do you really think she'd obey you just because you told her to?" Mijak's reasoning brought forward laughter from the students, and with the laughter came strength. One student realised that and pushed to the front. Brandon appeared next to Sophelia with his cousin Neoli.

"Sorry we're late, we were taking out the trash, though it looks like we missed a bit." Brandon laughed at his own joke, it may have been an old one but it didn't fail to make the students laugh. The joke had done its job, whilst the students laughed and the Dream Squad looked on in anger, Neoli had managed to make her way to Mijak, whispering something in his ear, he nodded solemnly, his expression changing from laughter to serious.

"Enough of this idle chit chat! Surrender now and I guarantee no harm will come to those who stand out here, I am not interested in those who can already control their hidden magic. However, fight and I will show you no mercy." Philon's voice cut through the laughter.

Before Alfred could speak up, Sophelia shouted at the person who called himself her best friend's father. Tears still streaming down her red cheeks, her hair a mess, but her voice was clear.

"Well come on then, we aren't cowards. If you want to take this school, and all our friends who aren't as skilled as us, you'll have to go through every single person here. We won't give up." The students cheered and clapped Sophelia, showing their support for what she had said.

"As you wish. Men! You may kill when needed, don't show them mercy, however, leave Alfred to me, I have a debt that I owe him. And as for my daughter, I would prefer her to live through this, I need a private word with her." Philon addressed his army, who roared in reply, eager to start the battle. The students matched their cheers with their own, putting on a brave face, before readying themselves for the upcoming fight.

There was a momentary calm, like the calm before a storm, then all hell broke loose. Different coloured balls of light flew through the sky from the Dream Squad at the students, who had erected shields surrounding themselves to protect from the onslaught. Then they charged, in the chaos Teara lost Sophelia and Alfred. Reaching for her dagger, in the hope that it would deter the enemy, she was grabbed roughly by her shoulders. Before she could grasp her dagger she was being pulled by two large, burly men. They were trying to drag her to the safety of the forest, away from where she wanted to be. Teara started thrashing and managed to lose one of the men, however he was soon up on his feet. Kicking her other captor in the face, Teara was once again free. But her joy was short lived as two more men, leaving there previous opponents in death chains, made their way over to her. Before they managed to trap her in a circle, Jessye and Neoli appeared on either side of her. Teara couldn't help but breathe a sigh of relief, there would have been no way she could have taken on those men by herself.

"We don't take kindly to people attacking our academy, or our friends!" Neoli shouted before screaming an incantation Teara had never heard, '*iomaduíl dom!*' Instantly three more Neoli's appeared, each one attacking an enemy, leaving Teara and Jessye in momentary peace.

"Here, let me take a look at that." Jessye grabbed Teara's hand and placed a finger on the slash there. She hadn't even realized she had been hurt. Briefly closing her eyes, Jessye moved her finger across the slash. Teara watched in wonder as the skin started to knit together, leaving nothing, not even a scar. Opening her eyes Jessye smiled at Teara, and placed a finger over her lips, signalling she wanted this to be kept a secret. Teara smiled as Jessye ran off. She wasn't the only one who had secrets. Somehow Jessye could heal without using the ancient words to harness her hidden magic.

Before Teara could think anymore a sharp scream beside her jerked her back to reality. One of the Neoli clones disintegrated. Running over Teara screamed '*Dóiteáin dragan anáil*'. She felt the heat as the flame left her mouth and landed on two of the men attacking Neoli, they immediately left the fighting and tried to stop the flames that were eating at their clothing. However for every man she defeated more seemed to take their place. It was almost like fighting a Hydra. Closing her eyes, Teara focused on the time she had fallen into an icy river, how the cold had spread quickly through her body, she recreated that feeling and spoke the words "*Sci stoirm nacht.*" The men who had been about to continue their onslaught on the nearby students had to quickly change their attack, in order to defend themselves from the pride of ice lions who were pouncing on them. Teara's eyes went bleary and she fell to the floor.

Opening her eyes she didn't know how long she had been out of it, but her lions were nowhere to be seen. The incantation had been too strong for her, moulding one creature was fine, two was ok, but a whole pride just took it out of her. Slowly making her way to her feet, she saw that the battle still raged. Jessye was flitting around healing people as fast as she could no longer caring that her secret was out. Whilst Neoli defended her from any attack. It was obvious the two were tiring and fast. Both had only ever practiced fighting whilst their enemy had been in multiple fights, as well as probably being highly trained by her father.

Turning her head she saw Brandon fighting three men, a slash in his head pouring blood across his face. He was making his usual wise cracks whilst fighting, goading his foes into getting angry, and in doing so make a mistake thus leaving an opening or which he could take advantage of.

Teara kept scanning the battle around her, looking for the one person she was most worried about. Finally she spotted her. Sophelia had teamed up with Mijak. Whilst Mijak was fighting the five men that were attacking them, Sophelia was defending herself and him from the attacks. Having Mijak on the offence and Sophelia on the defence, gave the two more chance of survival, as each only had to focus on one aspect of the fight instead of darting between the two. However it wasn't working as well as it should have, Sophelia was trying her best, but her right arm had been slashed, and she was limping on her right leg. The pain was hindering her concentration and due to that attacks kept slipping through.

Teara ran over to her friend and immediately started helping to keep up the defence. Sophelia smiled half-heartedly at her and nodded her head towards Mijak, signalling that she thought he was cute. Teara rolled her eyes at her. Even in a life and death situation, where Sophelia was badly injured and still fighting, she couldn't help but notice how good looking a boy was. If anything Teara believed it just showed how her friend was increasingly optimistic no matter how dark the outlook was.

"Get going and find Alfred!" Mijak ordered them, and the two girls immediately gave up their defensive positions and went in search of their headmaster.

Ducking and avoiding attacks they couldn't help but notice the blood spattered ground, where students and Dream Squad members alike lay screaming in pain. Fortunately, thought there seemed to be many injured, there wasn't one student who wasn't breathing. At that moment, the two girls had hope, if they could survive this long there was a chance they could win.

Those who were injured were staring in amazement at the powers being shown. Never before had they seen such speed, skill and stamina being used to control such strong magic. After all none of these students had ever witnessed a battle, they had read about them but a book could never do the horror, pain and surreal beauty justice.

Sophelia screamed, dragging Teara to follow her line of eyesight. Sophelia had spotted Philon who had used the same incantation Teara had seen Neoli use earlier. Two Philons were attacking the one Alfred and a third was creeping up behind him, oblivious, a large knife in his hand. Without thinking and with a large scream Teara threw herself in between her Father and the man she saw as her dad. Before she could utter a single incantation, or reach for her dagger, she was slammed aside by a very large creature.

Immediately after a long high pitched scream filled the air. The whole field froze. Alfred, Philon, every student and Dream Squad member turned to look at what had pushed Teara away. Nothing human could have made that scream. Only a creature of pure magic, pure love and pure innocence could have a death scream as beautiful and terrifying as that. Seeing the silver blood that speckled the ground around her, Teara feared the worst. Many creatures had silver blood and she hoped it was any of those, not the one that she feared it was. The large knock had been painful but familiar. With dread in her heart, Teara pulled herself to her feet, turning to see what creature was dying. Lying on the ground, breathing heavily, a large slash across his throat was a unicorn. But not just any unicorn. It was her unicorn. The scream had been Spirit. Her Spirit. Her beloved friend who she had grown up with. Teara threw herself beside him, cradling his head in her lap. Shaking her own head in disbelief. Murmuring no,no,no continuously.

"Invaders, leave now or face my wrath and perish." Rosemi's voice was filled with power, and as she was slowly lifted into the air, her power became palpable. She had stood idly by, watching in hidden distress as her charge was hurt, healed then hurt again. Now everything had changed. A magical creature had been hurt. And not just any creature, one who lived within her forest. Now she could join the fray.

Raising his hand, Philon and his squad disappeared, they knew better than to fight a nymph, especially one who was so angry. Students ran around healing one another, while Teara bent down next to Teara, tears once more rolling down her cheeks, mixing with the blood that seeped from her shoulder. Alfred to walked over and stood next to her whilst Rosemi placed a single hand on Teara's shoulder. Each giving their support as Teara said her final goodbye.

<Chapter 21>

Goodbye

The dark sky and the brewing storm finally broke, letting lose large droplets of rain that fell softly to the cold ground below. Night was slowly creeping upon the land, darkening the already grey sky as it claimed day for its own. The wind had died leaving nothing but the still air, only broken by the rain that passed through, the trees were silent, as was everything that surrounded the academy.

The remains of the battle could still be seen in the dim light. The last few injured being healed by their peers. The last couple of students who were trapped within the grasps of death chains were being released by their teachers. Students and teachers alike moving around silently, as if in a daze, as they started to fix the damage the battle had caused to one another.

However, in the middle of the field lay one group who were still. All looking down at the horrible sight that lay below them.

Teara was still leaning over her friend, his head in her lap, stroking his nose in comfort. The life was slowly draining from his body. His bright white glow now slowly fading. Alfred held Sophelia within a hug, comforting her as best as she could, tears rolling down his own cheeks. The nymphs had made a circle around the dying unicorn, holding hands whilst watching the traumatic scene unfold.

Rosemi knelt over the unicorn, a hand above the slash in his neck, from which his lifeblood was seeping. After a few moments she lowered her hand, shaking her head. There was no hope of being able to heal Spirit. Even she could not heal him, and after glancing to her side she knew why. Picking up the golden arrow that lay on the ground she knew why her powers of healing did not work. This arrow made of gold had been enchanted, but the questioned remained, who had fired it? Spirit was going to die, all help was beyond him now.

Seeing the shake of her head Teara cuddled Spirit even tighter, her whole body flinched in shock when she heard his voice enter her head, as if nothing was wrong.

"*It wasn't your father's attack I was defending you from, there is an unknown enemy in our midst. That arrow was not fired from the battlefield.*" Teara couldn't help but blink in shock. Trying to hold back her tears.

"Who?" She asked her friend. But her question would never be answered, for though Spirit tries, his voice could no longer reach Teara's mind. Teara watched as her beloved friend took one last deep breath, then as the air left his wounded body, his soul left this world. Teara looked at Alfred, begging him with her eyes for this to not be true, but the shake of his head crumbled any hope she had left. She lay her head against Spirit's still warm shoulder, feeling the tears well in her eyes, taking a slight comfort in the warmth that came from her dead friend. But even this small comfort was denied her, as Spirit's body started to disintegrate into sea form, then into white sparks.

Teara stood as she watched the sparks float up into the sky, as her friend disappeared forever. Tears streamed down her cheeks, no longer being able to keep them back, she let them flow freely.

"I am so sorry, Teara, I will make sure Philon pays for this." Alfred said, releasing Sophelia from the hug and clenching his fist in anger.

"No. It wasn't him. Someone else took a shot at me,

and Spirit took it for me. He saved my life, and I never got to thank him." Teara looked over to see the shock that lay within Alfred's face. Behind him stood Brandon, Jessye, Mijak, Sophelia, and Neoli, all looking as if they shouldn't be listening to the conversation. All looking nervous. All worried at how Teara would handle this death by the hands of her father.

"But who Teara...none of your father's men would dare to try and kill you, I think your just suffering from denial." Alfred replied. Teara felt a surge of rage at his words. How dare he say she was in denial!

"It was someone else, someone from our school, or if not. Then someone who could sneak in, use a death curse and sneak out again undetected." Teara spoke quietly, her voice eerily like her fathers.

"But who would do that?" Sophelia spoke quietly, not denying what her friend said wasn't true, but not completely believing it either.

"I don't know!" Teara waved her arms in exasperation. "Do you really think that if I did I would still be standing here? But I will say this. Whoever did it, I am not going to let them get away unpunished." Teara clenched her fists as the anger flowed through her. Sophelia took a step away from Teara in shock. There was something strange emanating from her friend. Something that didn't suit Teara's personality. Something dark and unnerving. Something Sophelia had never seen before. Rage. Pure unadulterated rage.

"But who would do such a thing?" She asked timidly.

"I told you, I don't know!" Teara snapped, "But I know someone who will." She made to run towards the forest, but Rosemi's hand on her arm stopped her.

"Let me go, I have some business to do." Teara snapped at the woman who had been like a mother to her.

"Teara, you can't just run off, especially with the way you're feeling at the moment." Alfred told her, but Teara didn't care.

"Watch me." She wrestled out of Rosemi's grasp and sprinted towards the forest, ignoring her friends as they called after her, she knew where she needed to go. She knew who would give her answers and she wasn't going to wait until she had calmed down to go see them. As she reached the forest, the familiar spiral of leaves encircled her, taking her to where she wanted.

***

Teara reappeared in the same misty clearing she had only left a month or so ago. The same opaque mist surrounded the clearing but Teara took no notice of her surroundings, instead she marched straight over to the rock that lay in the centre of the clearing, standing upon it she shouted, her voice echoing all around her.

"Feather! Feather! Don't pretend you can't hear me, I know you're here." Teara turned on the spot, her eyes searching the mist, until, about eight meters away the air shimmered. The mist parted and Feather glided through it, her feet barely touching the floor.

"What is it young one?" Feather asked. Teara's annoyance grew. Usually Feather's mystic tones calmed Teara but at this present moment in time it just annoyed her. How can anyone be so calm and mystic at a time like this?

"You! That's what it is." Her voice was exasperated. Feather sighed. If possible, this only served to annoy Teara even more.

"You told me there was a fight on the horizon, but you never said anything that it would be with the Dream Squad and not with a school bully, or that it was going to take place during school time. You forgot to mention that half the students who fought would get hurt and there was that little teeny-tiny detail that one of my best friends was going to die!" Teara was out of breath and now breathing heavily, trying to stop the tears that were still flowing down her face.

"Teara..." Feather started but was interrupted.

"No. I don't want to hear any of your excuses. I don't want the whole, 'if I told you I may have changed fate'. I don't want any of that stupid advice people give when something happens. I don't want any 'it was written in the stars' or 'it was the fates design.' I don't need to hear it." Teara turned her back on Feather, she was hyperventilating and didn't know how much longer she could keep herself together.

"Just tell me who tried to kill me. Who killed Spirit? Please." Teara whispered.

"I cannot say. The time is not yet right for you to know."

"But..."

"No, no buts. All I can tell you is this. Take it as a riddle or a prophecy, to be frank I don't care. Just remember it and don't try to understand it until you have control of your emotions;

A friend is an enemy,
An enemy is a friend,
When their two paths cross,
A life will bend,
The moon is the shortest way,
And it's princess will have the last say."

With that Feather began to disappear.

"No, wait...what does it mean?"

"You will learn young one...you will learn." Feather disappeared. Teara was left standing alone in the middle of the clearing, staring in bewilderment at the place where she had last seen Feather. Slowly she made her way through the riddle, memorising it as she did so. 'A friend is an enemy' the first person to come to mind was Vinnie. But that couldn't be right, she was mean but she wasn't evil, besides she wasn't even a friend. 'The moon is the shortest way and it's princess will have the last say.' The last part was even more confusing. What did the moon have to do with anything? How could a moon have a princess? And what would it have the 'last say' on?

Teara collapsed on the floor, her legs buckling beneath her. This was all too much for one day. She closed her eyes and wept. Maybe Alfred would have the answer, but then again, this was something she would rather keep to herself. But she had kept the impending fight to herself and what had that done. It had got her friend killed. Teara curled up and let the sobs envelope her.

<Chapter 22>

The End of Term

A week had passed since Philon's attempted takeover and the battle that took place at the academy. Any newcomer would never have guessed that the previous week, a battle for life and death has taken place on the grounds, for the students had cleared up well. If anything the school looked even better than it did before. This was due to Alfred taking advantage of the mess and not only having the grounds cleaned, but the whole school. The field had been neatly cut, the excess grass being turned into hay bundles to be used for the pets. The stone steps had been jet washed so they gleamed, the ivy around the oak door had been trimmed, getting rid of the wild look, and all the windows had been washed so they shined in the light.

Overall, one could say the effects of the battle had been minor on the academy. Those effects that did last were how people were treated. Jessye and Neoli were renowned as the deadly duo, as due to the two of them working together no one was lost. Jessye was revered by many for having healing powers that didn't need incantations to be harnessed, though Alfred speculated that this might be down to her heritage, which he decided he would look into.

Mijak was the new head battle strategist at the academy, on the off chance there would be another attack. There was word of him even being called to other academies to help them with a defence plan.

Many students had been taken out of the

academy by their parents, in the belief that if you split up the children mass kidnappings would be harder. However, this view was often disputed by many for it would be easier to pick off lone children than a school who stands strong together, as the academy did.

The greatest change for the students was the avoidance of two of their peers. Teara and Sophelia were treated like they had contracted some sort of plague. Sophelia was only avoided by association, if she hadn't of been Teara's best friend then things would have been different. Teara, on the other hand, was avoided because of her heritage. Some of the students were in awe of her, not understanding how she could deny and talk to her father the way she did. Some scared of how much she could be like her father, and refusing to get to know how on the off chance they were right. Others were worried. Worried that she would indeed turn over to her father's side, and in doing so, tell any defence plans they had in place to him.

In the end the majority of the students had been changed in some way by the battle. Teara's small circle of friends had grown, Jessye, Mijak and Neoli all admired her for not taking the easy option of just following her father. They respected her for who she was and cared for her because they liked her spirit. Mijak liked how Alfred confronted her and she would answer truthfully even if it was something she knew he wouldn't want to here. Jessye was glad that Teara did indeed keep her secret, even if it was for a couple minutes, it showed that Teara could be trusted, and in Jessye's opinion, very few people could be. Neoli admired the strength and selflessness Teara showed in battle, a trait that she greatly respected.

All of this made Teara happy, she enjoyed hanging out with all three of her new friends. But she couldn't help but think of Feather's warning. Could it have been about a friend she had yet to make, or one that already existed? She had yet to tell anyone of the prophecy/riddle. The only one she had ever confided all her secrets to was Spirit, but since his death, she had been feeling more and more lonely. Her heart felt as if a piece had been ripped out, like an empty void existed within her.

She couldn't even talk to Rosemi as a bitter anger still existed within her. She was angry that Rosemi didn't intervene sooner in the battle, in doing so she may have saved Spirit's life. Teara understood the nymph's laws, which they couldn't fight unless they themselves or a magical creature under their charge was in danger. But surely there were times when rules could be broken, surely it had been one of those times.

It was the last day of the academic year, and all the students were discussing the plans they had for the upcoming four week holiday. However, Teara sat in the corner. She never got involved in these conversations, even when people were talking to her, as every holiday that came she would send it the same way. She would spend the whole time on the grounds of the academy, rarely sneaking off to visit a random city, town or village. Though she had been told to expect visits from Mijak, Jessye, Brandon and Neoli, which were bound to lighten the load of boredom. All in all this summer holiday looked to be one of the best. The only thing that bothered her was Feather's riddle, and the fact that her father couldn't get it into his head that she wanted nothing to do with him, let alone live with him.

Sophelia had already made her plans, though she had yet to tell Teara them. For the first two weeks she was going to stay with Teara at the academy, whilst her parents went to visit family in France. She had already asked Alfred and had received his permission, both agreeing it would be a good surprise for Teara.

Alfred, who was taking the class, was siphoning through papers on the desk, looking up he saw the class was alight with laughter and anticipation at the impending holiday. However, scanning the room he came across two faces of concern. Teara and Sophelia had their heads together, whispering about something serious. Alfred couldn't help but wondered what had the two girls so worried, but he pushed it to the back of his mind. Teara would tell him, she always confided in him in her own time, didn't she?

Little did Alfred know that throughout the past year Teara had slowly been growing away from him. She had been keeping more and more important information to herself, not even confiding in Sophelia. Though she knew sooner or later she would have to, for she knew that keeping secrets from your best friend would only weaken the relationship.

Finally, the last bell of the day rang. The class cheered. The bell wouldn't ring again for another four weeks and until then, the students could do whatever they wished without worrying about assignments, homework or what classes they had to attend the next day. As the two friends exited the classroom they gave Alfred a small wave, receiving one in return. Once they had reached the bottom of the stairs, Sophelia turned to her friend.

"I'll come visit you in a couple of days, I want to

get all my chores done in one go."

"OK. And when you do I have something very important to tell you." Sophelia looked at her friend in puzzlement before shaking her head.

"You're so mysterious these days, Teara. It's like you're in a world of your own."

"I wish, you're the daydreamer not me," Teara laughed.

"I guess you're right." The two friends walked to the edge of the academy grounds, chatting about nothing. It was almost like old times. Before any of the trouble with Philon had started. The two girls said their goodbyes, hugged and Teara waved as she watched Sophelia leave.

A bright ball of green fire appeared in front of Teara and as it disappeared she caught the letter that fell from it. Her name emblazed in calligraphy on the front. Before she could think on who had sent it, she ripped the letter open.

My Dearest Daughter,

Things did not work out as well as I would have like them to last week. I will not give up hope that one day you will retrieve your senses and accept my most gracious offer of coming to live by my side. It pains me to say this, but if you do not... you will find out how cruel I can really be.

So her father had resorted to threats to try and get his way. Well it wouldn't work. Scrunching up the letter, Teara continued to wave to Sophelia, who was now a speck in the distance. She had four weeks of holiday. Four weeks she was going to use to continue her research on how to defeat her father. Four weeks for her to remember what it was like to be carefree. Four weeks that she would not let her father ruin.

To be continued

Acknowledgements

There are many people I would like to thank. First of all is Stace Pollard who designed my lovely back cover, her creativity and imagination really brought the Naturne to life. I would like to thank my beautiful model Sammy (Nightmareinwonderland) who put up with me complaining on the hours of stitching it took to sow on all those leaves for her dress. Thank you to Tonie, who proof read the first ever copy of the book, who enjoyed it and shouted at me for not writing fast enough, I'm as proud of her for reading a book as she is of me writing one. Thank you to one Paul Willows, my fight trainer and the inspiration for Philon, (he is really a big softy). A big thank you goes to Daniel and Sam at New Generation Publishing for all their help, without you this book would not exist. And thank you to my partner Byron Love who kept me from going insane. And I must make my final thanks to my mum, dad, sister and brother whom I begrudgingly love (And other than this, I will never say it again!) who all put up with my complaining whenever a character wouldn't do as they were told.

About the Author

Well what do I say about me? I wrote this book when I was 14 and considering that I am now 20 it really hasn't changed all that much. I tell you if you ever want to publish a book it is a long process, you have to keep persevering but whatever you do don't give up as in the end it is worth it. I come from a very weird family (probably due to them being Irish) and have spent my whole life in Plymouth, rarely leaving, (I know its sad). I was raised a Catholic and though I still practise my faith I am very liberal, often swaying towards the pagan ideologies and very occasionally Buddha, (This even confuses me so don't worry). I have lots of pets, and have never lived without one my entire life. I love anime, manga and cosplay. If I was a better artist this would have been a manga. I am a viking re-enactor. And spend much of my own summer in a field making sure men remember to eat and drink without stabbing each other in the bum with their swords, it is a very enjoyable past time, I even have my own fighting knives :). So yeah...that's me. I write, I fight, I occasionally sing (mostly in the shower) and even go out and cosplay. I hope you enjoyed my book, and Teara's adventures will continue in the next novel (well duh!)

Lightning Source UK Ltd.
Milton Keynes UK
UKOW02f0934300914

239406UK00002B/17/P